Costa Rican Adventure with Ben and Gretchen

Costa Rican Adventure with Ben and Gretchen

Kathy Carman Henderson

This book is a work of fiction. Names, characters, places, and incidents are the product of the author's imagination or are used fictitiously. Any resemblance to actual persons, living or dead, events, or locales is entirely coincidental.

Henderson, Kathy Carman
  Costa Rican Adventure with Ben and Gretchen
  1.   Fiction 2. Travel 3. Adventure 4. Costa Rica
  5. Christian Fiction

First Printing

Cover drawing by author

THANK YOU

Thank you to the friends and family who read, made corrections, and critiqued my book for me. Thank you to Iris and Tricia for their help with the Spanish language and with cultural issues. Thanks to Cheryl who told me that this was a story people would enjoy reading and that it had a lot of truth in it. Thanks to Dora Beth & Trish who said they had a hard time putting it down. Thanks to Tyrone who said that he was proud of me.

CHAPTER 1

Gretchen pulled down the sleeves of her light-weight jacket with a decided huff. "I have never been so humiliated in my life!" she grumbled, just loud enough for others to hear. Her short gray hair held a little bit of static and gave the impression that it, too, was upset. Ben trotted along just behind, smoothing down his sparse sandy hair and tucking his timeless white shirt into his dress pants. "Honey, are you O.K.? They did release you."

Gretchen let the tears of released tension slip down her cheeks. "Yes," she said barely above a whisper. "They did release me."

As they found their seat on the small aircraft, she heard one of her fellow passengers whisper to her seatmate, "Let's look into traveling by train next time."

One hour earlier the airport security officer looked apologetic while she firmly took hold of Gretchen's arm. Gretchen, who knew her better as the social studies teacher for South Des Moines County High, protested.

"I'm not going to bolt, Amanda. You can search my luggage and me if you have to. I know it's your job, though I don't have a clue as to why that alarm sounded when I walked through."

Amanda the guard cleared her throat, "Mrs. Parks," she said with impressive formality, "We are going to have to search you *thoroughly*. For your comfort we will be taking you to a private room. And, because I know you, another member of security will be present."

As Amanda led Gretchen away, her husband Ben followed. Amanda stopped. "I'm not sure whether you can come, Pastor Parks." Her voice was more apologetic than formal this time.

A uniformed young lady appeared at the door toward which they were heading and nodded. Amanda smiled a tight smile, "I guess you can come with us, Pastor."

"I should think so," blustered Ben. "She's my wife and if she's in trouble, I'm either responsible for it or need to help her out of it."

Gretchen shook her head slightly. "Not the time for a sermon, sweetheart. We'll just let them do their jobs."

Behind the closed door, both Gretchen and Ben submitted to one of the inconveniences of modern air travel. When the searches were completed, they were motioned to chairs.

Gretchen sighed softly. "Are we going to get to visit our son in Costa Rica today?"

Ben frowned. "We passed the search, didn't we?"

Amanda disappeared quietly out of the door leaving the Parks alone with the other security officer. The slender woman, who was somewhere in her late twenties or early thirties, pulled out an identification card which she passed first to Ben and then to Gretchen. Gretchen noted both the CIA identification and the name on the card. The name was Lydia Pool.

"I have a confession to make," Ms. Pool said. "We set off the security alarm on purpose to get you back here. We had to officially search you, but we'd already done a thorough background check. I can tell you, Mrs. Parks, the name of the reform school where you worked after you finished college; and, Rev. Parks, I can tell you who left before you finished your sermon last Sunday. I can also tell you that, in spite of the blustering out there, both of you can keep a straight face and not flinch when it is important to do so. Years in the service of your churches have given you plenty of practice in those skills."

Gretchen's eyes held both wonderment and curiosity as she glanced toward Ben. Ben had his hands together in front of his mouth, staring thoughtfully straight ahead.

"I am not a local airport security guard, I am ..."

"CIA," Ben finished for her.

"Yes, CIA," she finished. "You read my ID quickly and thoroughly, sir."

"Years of experience in Baptist churches," Gretchen explained.

There was a slight twinkle in the CIA agent's eyes. "Yes," she paused. "We need your services today – your country needs your services." She noted that Ben sat up a little straighter in his chair at those words, but Gretchen rolled her eyes. "It is a small task, and the worst is actually behind you. They are holding the plane for you at this moment, so you should be able to complete your trip as planned. In fact, it is your destination which caused you to be chosen.

"We need some information, in the form of a sealed envelope, to be delivered to an agent in San José. The agent who was to make the delivery has been identified by ... hostile persons. All of our agents available at this time are too well known in Central America. So, we checked airline schedules for someone going where we needed that envelope to go."

"And you came up with us," added Gretchen quietly.

"Exactly." The fact that you are leaving from a small airport we considered an asset. Both your professions and your ages are also. You will only be responsible for the envelope until you are ready to exit the airport. You will hand it to a man with a name tag saying 'Jesus,'" she pronounced it the Spanish way – Hay-ZOOS, "at the terminal bank and monetary exchange."

"Jesus, that's appropriate," mumbled Ben.

"We tried to pick a name that you could remember without writing it down," responded the agent.

Gretchen giggled.

The agent nodded. "Yes, we know that you frequently have to ask for help with your passwords to online accounts."

"We'll remember it," Gretchen said with a nod.

"Does that mean you will be our couriers?" asked the CIA agent.

Gretchen and Ben looked at each other. Ben shrugged. Gretchen cocked her head to one side and lifted her eyebrows. Ben turned toward the agent, "Can we talk in private for a minute?"

The agent silently left. Ben scooted his chair close to his wife's and took one hand in his. "Let's pray," he whispered. "God, it would appear to be a good thing to help our country, but we know things aren't always what they seem. Give us a clear indication if this is not something we should do, and – because the plane is waiting – could you make it quickly?"

They sat together silently for a bit, then Gretchen spoke. "Lord, I'm not getting any real reason not to do this. I've got an uncomfortable feeling, but anything out of the ordinary gives me that feeling." She looked up at Ben. "What about you, Ben?"

"Honestly, I'd like to do this." Ben smiled. "Maybe it's the old military man in me, but we can do this; and I think we should."

Gretchen returned the smile. "Then we will. God, be with us."

Just then the agent returned. Gretchen and Ben nodded their consent.

"Good," Agent Pool said. "Here are some things you may need. The envelope first." She helped Gretchen secure it inside her clothing. "Now, contingency supplies. We do not expect a problem, but have found problems are much smaller if we prepare for the unexpected." She handed Ben a cell phone. "Secure line. International capabilities. Set for

Costa Rica. Speed dial will get you the following: 1. American Embassy 2. me 3. your son Cal 4. a safe taxi 5. a good doctor 6. a secured hotel room 7. room service in that hotel 8. the airlines and 9. the equivalent of our 911 service."

CHAPTER 2

Gretchen and Ben sat in the very back of the twelve passenger plane holding hands, almost trembling in their excitement. Gretchen had the envelope pinned inside her pants with her knit shirt draped over it so it really wasn't noticeable. She also had some extra cash tucked into a double pocket she had created in her travel outfit. The plan was so simple that they should have been able to relax, but the fact that they couldn't talk about it made it hard.

Forty-five minutes later they were walking through the St. Louis airport toward their next flight. The enforced silence continued to keep Gretchen on edge. She knew that it would not do to act suspicious if they were to be successful couriers, so she excused herself to go to the restroom. They were just passing a family toilet, so she ducked in there while Ben watched their luggage.

Inside Gretchen took care of business, then she patted her cheeks with water as she stared into the mirror over the sink. She sighed. "God," she whispered, "this is hard. I usually talk things out when I'm nervous, and I can't even talk to Ben about this now – in a place we could conceivably be overheard. But I can talk to you. You know what is happening. You know whether we made the right decision in doing this – though I'm not sure how we would have refused. Help me to relax ... OK, I remember that I wasn't very relaxed on our last trip to visit our son. And everything worked out. Let me trust You in the midst of this – this adventure." Another big sigh and a strange little dance to release tension, then Gretchen opened the door and took her turn watching luggage.

Ben had a slightly different ritual. He did his nervous dance first. Then he leaned his back against the door, lifted his hands over his head and stood there quietly for several moments. Breathing out slowly, he hummed a hymn as he finished his business.

The flight to Dallas-Forth Worth took about eighty minutes. The bathroom prayers had done their jobs enough that both Parks nodded off for a while. The three hour layover in Texas tested both of their calm. It was tested even more by an hour and fifteen minute delay before takeoff.

They watched a good movie on the flight, ate sandwiches, and filled out immigration forms. It was after eleven p.m. local time when they landed at Juan Santamaria International Airport outside the capital of Costa Rica, but still the same Tuesday in July that they had started out. Ben pulled down their carryon bags and they rolled them up the ramp through the Gate 1 door. Following a long line of fellow travelers, the clicking of shoes and the hum of wheels on a tiled surface announced their arrival.

Gretchen & Ben ducked into a restroom along the way, remembering to trash the toilet paper. When they got to the immigration lines, they were glad they had made the stop. Apparently because of the delay, their arrival was past the time most officials usually went home. There was a very long line in the room and only six people checking passports and luggage declarations.

All of a sudden Gretchen remembered a phone conversation of a couple of weeks ago with a friend from a former church. She tugged on Ben's sleeve as she searched the room. "When did I say the Workmans were coming to Costa Rica? Was it the same day as us?"

Ben frowned thoughtfully. "It seems like it was a couple of days later, though I'm sure you said something like 'Maybe we'll run into each other' when you were talking to Kitty."

Gretchen quit searching the crowd. "Well, they won

that special tour and we're just penny-pinching it with our college student. We probably won't be moving in the same circles."

Ben shrugged. "It's a small country. Who knows?"

It was time for them to grab their bags and roll.

"*Buenos di- Buenas noches*," said Gretchen as they maneuvered their luggage through the narrow channel next to one immigration desk.

"Passport, please."

Ben handed over his.

"Where will you be staying while in Costa Rica?" asked the young man behind the desk.

"*Con mi hijo*," replied Ben. "With our son."

The official returned Ben's passport and held a hand out for Gretchen's.

"Have you been in Costa Rica within the last six months?" he asked her.

"No, it's been a year," she said.

"And where does your son live?"

"Close to the University in San Pedro," Both replied almost in unison.

The man nodded and returned Gretchen's passport.

Ben and Gretchen rolled ahead to the escalator. They maneuvered their carryon bags on and off of that, and wove between people who were waiting for checked baggage. Gretchen noticed Ben start to stride forward at an increased speed, but she suddenly stopped in her tracks.

"Ben."

He turned and rolled back toward her.

"Ben, I've got to go to the restroom again," Gretchen murmured.

Looking concerned, Ben asked, "Problems?"

"I forgot something at the last one."

Understanding dawned on his face. Ben pointed to a sign across the large room: MUJERES. Gretchen scurried off. Inside a stall, Gretchen carefully unpinned the sealed letter and transferred it to her purse.

Returning to Ben, they rolled toward the luggage checkpoint. No, they had no food or commercial items with them. Suddenly the scanner started beeping loudly. The conveyer belt stopped. Gretchen and Ben watched the officer who had been talking to them hurry toward a young man they remembered from their plane. Gretchen unconsciously hugged her purse tighter. Another official waved Ben, Gretchen, and their luggage on. Gretchen glanced back at the young man who was being held at a distance as his luggage was searched by hand.

To the end of the hall; turn the corner. At the end of the long hall they could see eager people watching through a large window. Coming closer they saw their son Calvin waving. They waved in return. To the right was the last hurdle to exit the airport, passing one last set of officials, these in charge of transporting luggage out of the terminal, if help was needed. To the left was the airport bank and currency exchange. It was almost midnight; had they missed their connection?

Gretchen and Ben turned toward the bank. Out of the corner of their eyes they could see Calvin shaking his head and trying to get their attention. Both determinedly ignored his efforts. They very clearly remembered Calvin's instructions the first time they visited him: "Don't exchange money at the airport bank. The exchange rate is lousy. We can stop at an ATH, the same as your ATMs."

There was now tapping on the glass behind them. They looked for a person with JESUS on his nametag. All the people behind the counter were women. Gretchen's eyebrows went up as she looked at Ben. Ben glanced her way and pretended to study the posted exchange rate.

"May we help you?" One of the young women in the bank spoke.

Ben replied, "I think so, but first I would like to ask about someone who helped us a lot on a previous visit. Is

Hay-ZOOS (Jesus) working today?"

The women stared at each other blankly.

CHAPTER 3

A very smartly dressed young man hurriedly came through a door in the back. "Did I hear my name?" He said in clear, crisp English. His name tag read JESUS.

The young man was removing a satchel from around his waist, under his suit jacket. "I know it's unusual to get a visit from the main office at this time of night, but we heard that a late flight was coming in and were not sure that you would have on hand the *colones* to meet your needs."

He looked up, smiled brightly around at the young women and then apparently spied the Parks standing behind the counter. "Oh, *Señor y Señora* Parks! Calvin told me you were coming for a visit, but I did not know it was tonight! *Como estan?* How was your flight?"

"The flight was fine," answered Ben, "and we are OK."

"Yes, Calvin, is right outside the window waiting for us. He has told us not to use this bank, because the exchange rate is not good, so he may not look happy right now." Gretchen said with some emphasis.

Jesus looked out the window. Ben and Gretchen turned and saw Calvin, being restrained by an officer, just a little to the back of the group of people. Gretchen pointed to him and Jesus waved. Calvin automatically responded to the wave, though he looked confused.

"Give me your dollars, and we will make a good exchange rate for you," Jesus assured them.

Gretchen reached into her purse and drew out the envelope and handed it to Jesus. Jesus ripped one end of the envelope open, drew out a few bills that were inside and

11

dropped the envelope, apparently into the trash. Gretchen and Ben schooled their faces not to show surprise.

"Here you are, *mis amigos*," said Jesus as he handed them a good sized stack of colones, in a variety of denominations and also including a handful of coins. "Give my best to your son," He said with a flourish of friendly dismissal.

Gretchen and Ben turned toward the terminal exit. Behind them they could hear Jesus saying, "Let us get the money I brought sorted out. Some of it I will lock up for the early morning flights."

In a minute they were outside, being greeted by Calvin in a rather abrupt way. "Mom, Dad, it's good to see you; but what was that all about?"

"We know you told us not to use that bank, but it's the middle of the night – not a good time to stop at an ATM," Ben replied.

"It is good to see you, too," Gretchen responded as they hurried away towards Calvin's car parked just across the road in the airport garage. Since they were traveling light, it only took a moment to load the car and get on their way.

Out on the road, they had time to notice the clear night and the scattered lights on the hills around Costa Rica's Central Valley. Those lights mimicked the stars that were shining above. The traffic wasn't bad and the highway was in good repair, so they made good time as they circled the capital city.

"Something strange was going on back there in the terminal with you and that banker," Calvin said after a while. "Can you tell me what it was about?"

Both Ben and Gretchen were quiet. Finally Ben responded, "I'm not sure that we should, Calvin."

Calvin laughed. "You'll have me thinking my parents are spies or something if you act so mysterious about it."

Gretchen chuckled nervously. Calvin glanced at her in his rearview mirror. "Now you really have me wondering!"

Ben cleared his throat. "Well, Gretchen, it is over. We've fulfilled our instructions, even if they threw it in the trash."

"The trash?" questioned Calvin.

Gretchen put a hand on his shoulder. "Pay attention to your driving, Cal. We're not spies, but we were asked to carry a message and leave it with a particular person in the airport."

Calvin's eyes got wide, but did as his mother told him and focused on his driving. Calvin's apartment was just a couple of blocks from the University of Costa Rica campus in San Pedro on a narrow street filled with a wide variety of busy little shops. He turned into a drive which seemed barely wide enough for a car to fit through. Then he stopped, unlocked a gate and pushed it to one side. Ben got out, too, and pulled the gate closed as soon as Calvin had driven the car through.

A sharp turn to the right brought them to a parking place exactly 15 inches wider than the car. Gretchen got out before Calvin parked, so he could leave three inches on the right side and have a foot to squeeze out on the left. There was a steep set of outdoor stairs running up the right side of the parking area, and they all ascended, lugging suitcases along with them.

Calvin's was the first door at the top of the stairs. He unlocked an iron grill and swung it open, blocking the second floor walkway continuing beyond his door. Next, he unlocked his solid wooden door by the light of a single small bulb set at the top of the stairs. Inside, his ten-by-twelve living room/dining room/kitchen quickly transformed from a spooky closet to a room crossed with deep shadows cast by the bulb mounted in the center of the ceiling. He and Ben took the bags to the bedroom and deposited them next to a comfortable double bed.

Gretchen looked around and noticed that Cal had already made up the living room futon as his bed, and had moved a small night stand next to it to hold a few of his things. It looked like the setup would be about the same as the previous year. She walked to the kitchen cupboard and pulled out three glasses marked: ME, MY MOM, and MY DAD. These would be their personal glasses for the week. Calvin had two more for company. Going to the refrigerator, she pulled out a gallon jug of water and poured a half glass for each of them. Calvin and Ben came out of the bedroom and accepted their glasses gratefully.

"What's the plan?" Gretchen asked.

"Tonight I want more of an explanation from my mother the spy," said Cal with a grin. "Tomorrow we can go over to the campus to get my semester grades," he grimaced and then smiled. "Then we can have some fun."

Gretchen's mouth made a firm line. She glanced at Ben.

Ben sighed. "Since it is over, and it was a one-time thing, I think it's OK to tell you a little more about our travel adventure." He spoke in a low voice that would not accidentally travel through the building's thin walls. "We were detained as we tried to board our first plane on the excuse that something had set off the security alarms."

Gretchen took over the story, keeping her voice down, too. "A courier for the CIA had been identified at the last minute; others were already too well known; we were picked from among travelers going to Costa Rica from the Midwest today."

"Just an envelope to a young man in the airport bank. That's it," said Ben, spreading his hands in finality. "We handed the envelope to a man with a nametag which said 'JESUS.' There was US currency inside, along with whatever message was being sent. The bank man, gave us a stack of *colones* in return and appeared to throw the envelope away."

"That puzzled us," said Gretchen, "But we had done our job, so we just went ahead and left. "You know the rest."

Calvin looked confused. "What you say makes some sense," he concluded, "but I've never heard anything like it before."

"I imagine that most of what the CIA does we've never heard of before," said Ben.

Calvin chuckled. "You're probably right." He yawned. "Let's get some sleep."

Ben and Gretchen heard Calvin puttering around before seven the next morning, Wednesday. The door opened, closed, and then opened again a short time later. With the second opening, came the odor of fresh-baked bread. "Carmen's bakery," mumbled Ben.

Gretchen grunted in reply. They dozed off again, but were awakened by a persistent banging.

"What is Calvin doing?" asked Gretchen, rising to one elbow.

Ben flipped off the covers and reached for his pants. "I don't know, but I think this is our signal to get up."

From the other room they heard the click of a deadbolt lock being opened. "What?" This brief exclamation came from Cal.

"Calvin Parks?" The name was spoken in syllables so precise they could not have been from a native English speaker.

"Yes."

"I am Jesus. Did your parents mention..." There was a clanging from the iron bars which formed the outer barrier to the apartment.

Ben dashed from the room as Gretchen shrugged on her outer garments. Ben saw Calvin struggling to help the young man from the bank inside the room and over to the futon. Ben hurried to help, his brow furrowed.

"Jesus, what's happened?" Ben asked.

"Turn on the TV, *señor*."

Cal turned to the small flat screen he had hanging on

one wall. As the screen lit up, a pretty dark haired lady with generous cleavage was looking more serious than Ben and Gretchen remembered her being about the news last year. They scanned the English subtitles as the woman spoke in Spanish. "... late last night at the airport bank. The man who had been posing as a bank employee is not only missing but believed to be injured. He took an undetermined amount of cash. Bank officials are checking yesterday's records to figure out what was taken."

Gretchen turned back to the man lying on the futon. Calvin was using bottled water to wipe blood from his head very gently. "Who are you?" she asked.

"Like you, I was doing a job for the CIA," replied Jesus. He sat up a little straighter and continued. "I actually am on loan to that organization from a counterpart in a – another country in the Americas ... to help in the battle against drugs in your country."

Both Gretchen and Ben looked grim. Ben said, "We want to hear more, but first – how are you feeling?"

"Not well, *Señor* Parks, but some rest and – and – pardon for the request – some food will help considerably."

Calvin went back to the kitchen and put a thick slice of fresh bread, spread with butter, on a small plate. Then he poured a mug of *horchata de arróz*. He set both on the night stand next to Jesus. Jesus picked up the sweet drink and drank slowly and deeply. Then he leaned back and closed his eyes for a moment.

Opening his eyes again, Jesus sipped a little more of the traditional rice beverage, before speaking again. "I will try to tell you the story of last night as briefly as I can without missing important details. This may seem all very irregular, but right now you are the people I trust most, so please listen!"

Calvin was watching this exchange and saw his parents nod while frowning deeply. This was the very expression they had when he asked his parents to believe him over apparent evidence to the contrary.

"I got a message that I was supposed to exchange some *colones* for an envelope from a mature U.S. couple who would be arriving some time after eleven p.m. When I started for the airport, I thought I was being followed, so I ditched my car and took a cab. This process made me later than I planned on being, and I was very afraid that I would have missed my contact – you.

"My understanding was that the bank outlet would actually be closed. It was supposed to close at about 10 p.m. on the usual night. So, I was not only wondering if I had missed you but wondering why there were four women tellers at a facility usually only staffed by two people during its regular business times. I took your envelope, gave you the money, with the paper I had taken out of the envelope along with your money. I had not read the paper, but did not think I should keep it in my possession with the four unexplained women present."

Gretchen opened her mouth to speak.

"I used to work as a magician, so it was a simple slight-of-hand trick."

"That makes sense," she responded. Ben got up and quietly walked into the next room.

"As you left, I turned to the women, continuing to pretend that I was a bank official bringing money for the next day's business." I started to speak to three of them while wondering what had happened to the fourth. A sharp pain to the back of my skull answered that question. When I woke up later, a night maintenance worker was shining a light in my eyes.

"Later, after an examination by an emergency room doctor, I heard the medical staff talking down the hall about police being called because I was probably a bank robber. Since I was in a position which made it difficult to explain myself, I decided to leave without telling anyone.

"Part of my information about my contacts that night

was about their son. Since I had put the message I was supposed to receive back in their possession ...."

"Oh!" Gretchen jumped up.

Ben walked back into the room, waving a paper. "In our possession," he repeated.

All eyes turned to the paper.

CHAPTER 4

A serious young woman turned from her wardrobe full of uniforms for a variety of professions to the morning news. It was tuned to a channel from Central America. Because of the late arrival of the Parks' plane, the chances of any breaking news related to yesterday's message was slim; but she did not want to miss it, if it was there.

The reporter was speaking in Spanish, but she had tuned in English subtitles. "Overnight excitement at the airport banking branch has that facility still closed this morning. An unconscious man was found by a custodian on the floor inside that facility during the night. He was taken to a hospital for treatment, but disappeared from the examining room. It is reported that a robbery took place at that facility, and the police are seeking this man as a person of interest."

The young woman had her secure cell phone in her hand by this time, speed-dialing her superior. "Lydia Pool here, sir. I think there has been a major glitch in the Parks plan." She listened for a moment and then responded. "I am always packed, sir. I will pick up my tropical suitcase and be at the airport within the hour. Am I to call them?"
***

At that moment Ben reached for his cell phone. He glanced at Gretchen. "Who do I call?"

"Why don't we start with Ms. Pool," replied Gretchen. "There will be less explaining to do talking to her than with anyone else."

Ben dialed.

Lydia had just hung up when her phone rang. Glancing at the number, she breathed a sigh of relief. Her superior had said not to call the Parks, and she had felt uncomfortable with that. "Yes." she answered the phone with no more greeting than that, in case the phone was not in the Parks' hands.

"Ben Parks here. This job you gave us has become more complicated," he said. "We have the note, the money, and your man all in our possession and we don't know what to do with any of them," he stated bluntly.

"You have what – who?" stuttered Lydia.

"Jesus knew he was walking into a trap last night, so he changed up the agenda. It may have saved the day, but didn't help keep him in one piece," continued Ben cryptically.

"The line is secure. Your can speak plainly," Lydia said.

"Good," said Ben, but lowered his voice. "But our walls are thin. Can you hear me now?"

"Affirmative."

"I think I will let you talk to Jesus."

Jesus explained the situation much like he had explained it to them. Cal was the one who noticed Jesus' pallor.

Ben took the phone back. "If we can continue the conversation, Jesus has had a rough night and probably should be in the hospital. It would be better if he rests."

Lydia agreed. "I am on my way to you. My plane should arrive in about five and a half hours. I will be posing as your daughter and will stay with you until this all is sorted out.

"What you need to do now is call the embassy and ask for a ride for your party. Then call the hotel line and ask for the Americas suite for your party for the next three nights. If this gets worked out quickly, you will have the suite at your disposal and it is close to several tourist attractions."

Ben did as he was told. Then everyone packed for a

three day trip. Ben stuffed the CIA's message in his inside jacket pocket. Within half an hour a red van stopped outside. A call came through on Ben's phone. "Everyone is to get in the red van. It will take you to the U.S. embassy until your contact arrives."

En route, the phone rang again. "Lydia here, Dad," she said, getting into character. "Uncle Sam says you are to ask the secretary to send in Jerry as soon as possible and to contact the drug task force."

Within 10 minutes of their arrival at the embassy, Jerry, the resident decoder, was studying the document which the Parks had brought from Iowa the day before. His mouth became grim as he jotted down a few cryptic notes. Five minutes later two Latino-looking people entered the room. Jerry glanced at them and then around the room. "Should we find another spot to talk?"

The men shook their heads. "Inadvertently we have embroiled the Parks and Señor Caldarón much more than was first intended. They may need to know what is happening for their own safety."

Ben and Gretchen were staring at the man who had identified himself as Jesus. "If you don't mind, Jesus Caldarón is as good a name as any for today."

Ben and Gretchen nodded. Calvin, who had been uncharacteristically quiet, said, "For our safety?"

The two Hispanic-looking men nodded, "Your parents were only supposed to relay a name and a time to – uh – Jesus, who was then supposed to relay it to our task force. With the complication of the late night bank robbery, you all may be in some danger.

"We are working hard to find the female robbers and to determine if they were simply robbers or if our total plan has in some way been compromised. In the meantime, you have been able to deliver the message..." Jerry nodded in confirmation. "... and it will soon be on its way to our team."

At this point one of the two men consulted in low voices with Jerry and then with someone else over the phone. The other man continued, "Until we find the women robbers and know for sure what their intentions were, we are putting the four of you in protective custody. You have made a hotel reservation?"

All nodded.

"Good. The rooms around yours will either be empty or have a variety of civil servants in them. It is a beautiful location, so the limitations should be somewhat made up for by the vacation atmosphere."

CHAPTER 5

The next morning, Thursday, when Gretchen came out of the bedroom she was sharing with Ben, she noticed Lydia hunched over a small laptop listening to something with earphones. When Lydia saw Gretchen, she punched a button on the remote laying before her on the table and the room's television lit up. Gretchen again watched the buxom newscaster and scanned the translated captioning below. "This all happened late yesterday. The cocaine which was captured is now in the custody of the U.S./Costa Rican united drug unit. Several people are in jail this morning awaiting formal charges. Unfortunately, the U.S. tourist who was the courier for the drug cartel did not survive his wounds. Here is a statement from the spokesman for the drug task force."

"We are saddened by the death of this man who apparently was tempted into being a courier by financial reversals during the last year. However, we hope that he has not died in vain – that his death will discourage other people in both of our countries from getting involved in the drug trade."

Gretchen turned to Lydia. "Is that it then? Is it over?"

"We have not caught the women bank robbers yet," Lydia reminded her. "And we know that the man who died was a very small fish. He was a last minute substitute, which makes us think that our hand was tipped."

Ben came out, scratching his grizzled head. "So, are we locked in our rooms? Or can we go swimming?"

Lydia laughed. "We'll order in breakfast, get a report from those in and out of the hotel, and make that decision.

Our van is here. Our driver is in an adjacent room if we need him."

"In the meantime, I'm going to take a shower," said Ben, disappearing back into the bedroom."

"And I'm going to get settled," declared Gretchen. "I hate having to paw through a suitcase every time I need something." She too disappeared.

Lydia could occasionally hear a snort coming from the men's room which told her that they had not awakened yet. There was both an oven and microwave in the suite, so she went ahead and ordered a large Costa Rican breakfast for everyone. Next she quietly folded the sheets she had used the night before and set up the hide-a-bed for day use. She had expected the breakfast to take some time to arrive, but it came before Ben or Gretchen returned to the suite's common area.

Two slender young dark-haired maids entered the room after knocking and announcing that they were "room service." It may have surprised them to see one lone female occupying the largest suite the hotel had, for they glanced around in wonder. Lydia pointed to the sideboard, and they laid out trays of melon and pineapple, fresh bread, and rice and beans. There was also a bowl of scrambled eggs and some slivers of ham. The aroma of coffee filled the room from one pitcher, while another was clearly filled with some kind of juice.

"*Muchas gracias,*" Lydia said with a decidedly U.S. accent as she slipped each one a 100 *colones* coin (about twenty cents). The maids looked affronted at the size of the tip, but forced smiles as they slipped from the room. Lydia hoped she gave the impression of an ignorant first-time visitor.

Just as the suite door closed, Calvin opened the door from his room sniffing the coffee.

Lydia looked at the young man and caught herself thinking how much like a child he seemed. She knew he must be about twenty and very able to take care of himself, but his tousled hair, casual jeans, T-shirt, and flip-flops all gave the appearance of a teenager on vacation with his parents.

"I love this Costa Rican coffee!" he stated with enthusiasm. "And, surprisingly, their rice and beans."

Lydia smiled because she felt the same, but she was on duty, not on vacation. "How is Jesus?" she asked.

"Stirring. He will probably be up soon. He slept like a log. So sound that I checked him to see if he was breathing once."

Lydia nodded. She had had dealings with the man they were calling Jesus once before. He seemed to be a competent agent and a decent person, but it was always hard to tell with people whose job it was to assume various identities. He could certainly be charming.

"You're smiling," commented Cal. "What thought brought that on?"

Lydia grinned bigger. "I was just thinking about the fact that this assignment included guarding two handsome young men."

Cal grinned back. "Guarding us? I thought we all were guarding Mom and Dad."

Lydia lowered her voice in reply. "I hope the guarding is almost over."

Cal lifted his eyebrows.

"The drug deal has gone down, with police interference; but the lady bank robbers have not been located yet, so ..."

"Breakfast in our suite, I see," finished Calvin.

Lydia nodded.

Lydia, Calvin, and even Jesus had finished their breakfast before Ben and Gretchen joined them in the main room. Lydia was getting just a little concerned. "What is keeping them?" she asked Calvin.

Calvin shook his head in response as he got up and moved toward their door.

Almost under his breath Jesus replied in one word, "Prayer."

Calvin looked quickly at Jesus with his mouth open. He pushed open the door a few inches and let it drop closed, nodding.

"Of course Jesus is right," Calvin said in a quiet voice. "I should have known. Difficult situation equals extra time in prayer."

Lydia looked somewhat baffled.

Cal smiled brightly at her. "They have probably been praying for your safety, your family, and your wisdom in making decisions today, as well as for themselves."

Jesus added, "*En el nombre de Jesus y el poder de ese nombre!*"

"Exactly," Calvin agreed. "In the name of Jesus and the power of that name."

"Oh, that's right," Lydia said suddenly. "Ben is a preacher."

Cal chuckled, "It has less to do with his job and more to do with his relationship with God. He talks to him constantly, whatever is going on."

The door opened and Gretchen and Ben walked out looking refreshed.

"*Señor* Parks," said Jesus. "Any time you want to include us in your prayer sessions, please do!"

Ben's face lit up. "Thank you, Jesus. So you are a praying man!"

"*Sí, señor,*" I did a lot of praying between midnight and seven on the night you arrived in Costa Rica, but I pray when I'm not beat up and lost also."

"That is good to hear," said Gretchen. "You have access to God's direction then, as well as your training."

Lydia listened quietly to this interchange. She was not going to say anything to disparage the faith of these people, but she found it a distraction. All her senses needed to be on the alert to any possible problems. Though God was very good in His place, she was sure, she could not afford to turn her attention from present realities. She herself had fond memories of Vacation Bible Schools and singing Bible songs in Sunday School. This God could make her feel warm and fuzzy, but warm and fuzzy would not keep these people safe. She set about warming up the eggs and rice for the Parks.

CHAPTER 6

Lydia sat stewing in the van, wishing that she had not let Cal return to the suite alone for his camera. She had consulted with superiors, and they felt that everyone might actually be safer on the move. In fact, it would look very unnatural for a family newly arrived in Costa Rica to spend the day in a hotel room. So, they were going volcano hopping today.

Everyone had been securely stowed in the minivan with Jaime, their driver, when Cal slipped from his seatbelt while saying, "Forgot the camera. Got to get some pictures of Mom's expressions as the lava flows around her." He winked and disappeared inside. When he returned, he held up the camera before slipping it into his pocket. "Got it," he said. "And just in time to tell the maid that we didn't need any service today. I took the towels and said *no gracias* to anything else."

Jesus, sitting next to the driver, scowled. The driver started the engine and pulled out of the driveway. Lydia was frowning also. Jesus saw the frown in the sunshade mirror; he swung around and asked, "Didn't you tell the hotel that we would not need maid service today."

"I certainly did. I said that someone would ask if we needed or wanted anything."

"Then who was the woman at the door when Cal showed up?"

Lydia was on the phone before Jesus finished his sentence. Gretchen and Ben quietly prayed in the third seat. They continued on down the highway, passed through a heavily congested community, and started climbing a winding mountain road. Lydia's phone rang. She listened, asked a couple of questions, and then put the phone away.

"Two women in custody. The two who brought our breakfast, one of whom returned with the towels." She looked seriously at the back of Jesus' head. "Jesus, do you think you would recognize your attackers?"

"Maybe. They were good-looking professional young Latin women. Not too many distinguishing marks, and I was concentrating on the Parks. However, since I was surprised by their presence, I tried to take a quick, thorough look."

"We will try to have a lineup for you by tonight."

Jesus nodded. The driver Jaime continued up the mountain. Recent rains had caused the outside lane of the road to be washed down the hillside. Traffic was backed up while a police officer waved sections of cars through, first from one direction and then the other. They made it through the damaged section of the road and soon came to a small community.

Jesus suggested they stop at a *Farmacia* and get drinks for everyone. Only he got out and came back with bottled water and a variety of soft drinks. He frowned as he looked out the back window. "Did you see a brown car behind us shortly after we left the hotel?" he asked, looking first at Lydia and then at the driver. Both nodded. "Well, there is a brown car parked about a block behind us. Looks like the same car."

The driver spoke. "Let's see what happens now." He started their vehicle and pulled into traffic. Behind them, the brown car also pulled into traffic. They continued to weave through the town and the brown car matched them turn for turn until just before they drove out into the country again. The brown car pulled into a winding dirt road which led to a small house on the hillside. Everyone breathed a sigh of relief.

Along the roadside, farm fields gave way to forests.

The atmosphere became misty, almost cloud-like. Soon they passed a sign announcing a national park and the Poas Volcano ahead. A few miles on down the road, the beautiful forest parted to reveal a long parking lot. The driver did not hurry to park, but made a tour of the long lot before selecting a place between two cars with baby seats in the back of each.

As they unloaded, Lydia commented to the driver, "You know you've put your van in danger of being dinged. Little kids. People won't be staying too long."

Jaime shrugged. "I'm not worried about dings."

Gretchen and Ben forgot all of the events of the last couple of days as they marveled at their surroundings. They called to Calvin to help them with the names of various exotic plants. When Cal didn't know, they turned to Jesus. He smiled and entered into this activity, playing the tour guide even to the point of reciting common stories about the history and uses of various plants.

Lydia hung back just a little with the driver Jamie, keeping a lookout for anyone who seemed to be giving the group more than passing attention. At this point, there was no one. She relaxed ever so slightly.

They passed the gift shop and museum and headed in the direction of the volcano's main crater. All up hill, the wide lane continued to be lined with a variety of exotic foliage. One of the most common was a plant commonly called the Poor Man's Umbrella, a plant with leaves measuring two feet or more across. A variety of flowering bushes and delicate orchids also decorated their way. The party moved from one beautiful plant to another until fog began to make seeing more than a few feet ahead difficult.

Lydia and Jamie closed ranks with the rest of the group. It was Jesus who said, "In case we get separated, just keep going up until you reach a flat, fenced in area. That will be the viewing station for *Laguna Caliente*, the lake which fills the main crater."

"Is there any point in going up, if it is going to be foggy like this?" asked Ben.

Jaime the driver spoke, "I have heard a phrase: 'Wait for it.' This applies to Poas. A breeze will come down the mountain and the fog will be blown away. I have never been here that this did not eventually happen, though I have had to wait almost half an hour at times."

Jesus continued. "If we decide to go along to the upper crater, once you pass that lake, the rule is to keep following the path. It will eventually bring you back to the main lane."

"That's good to know," said Gretchen, "Though I intend to stick close to all of you, if possible."

Lydia grinned. "Good idea."

Just as they reached the viewing area, the breeze which the driver had spoken of blew over them all. The fog followed the wind and everyone who had been waiting in the viewing area let out a gasp at the brilliant green water below them. Along the side of the lake, small fumaroles spewed steam. These were marked by variously colored deposits around the openings. Ben noted a distinct sulfur smell permeating the air.

Lydia watched the crowd, rather obvious about what she was doing. Jaime lounged to the back of the group, looking bored; but actually watching as closely as Lydia. During the half hour spent at this spot, the lake began to change color. The water's green color became less intense. It was almost like milk being poured into a green drink. Then the fog began to return, and with it an even stronger sulfur smell.

The group circled. "Do we go back to the gift shop and museum or go on and up?" asked Lydia.

"What recommendations do you all have?" asked Ben.

Cal spoke up. "The trail is steep, but beautiful. You should be able to handle it unless you are having some type of leg or foot problems."

"I'm good," said Ben.

"Me too," responded Gretchen. "If it is permissible, I would like to walk through the cloud forest. That was on my to-do list for this visit with Calvin."

Jesus grinned. He turned to Lydia. "I like these people." He turned toward the Parks. "Will you adopt me, *por favor?*"

Gretchen and Ben chuckled. "We would discuss any adoptions with the son we already have," replied Ben.

Calvin smiled, but did not reply. He was seeing a new side of his parents which he had never been aware of before.

Many of the approximately fifty people who had been watching *Laguna Caliente* turned to go back down the road toward the gift shop, but about fifteen besides themselves turned toward the uphill path. Happy chatter could be heard coming from the various groups. When they reached the upper crater, this pool was still shrouded in mist. They sat down on some of the benches surrounding this scenic spot. Cal talked about some of the other sites in Costa Rica that he would like to show his parents. He addressed some of his remarks to Lydia since she seemed to be in charge.

"Last year I took Mom and Dad to Jaco for a beach experience."

"Did you go surfing *con sus padres?*" asked Jesus.

Gretchen chuckled, but let Cal reply.

"Not quite," replied Calvin, "But we did chase a surf board which had escaped its owner."

"And we did not stay in one of the shared room hostels," added Ben. "I draw the line with sharing my snoring with strangers."

"Though I did suggest it, if money was a problem."

Gretchen added, "Ben is so tight sometimes that I was almost surprised that the twelve dollars per night cost did not tempt him."

Lydia rubbed her hand over her face. She must stay alert about their surroundings. There was a couple on the bench closest to the path who seemed to be glancing their way more than one would expect. "If the fog doesn't clear within 5 minutes, Cal, I suggest we take the folks on down and head for Arenal."

The rest of the group looked at her and wondered why she was changing the plan to walk through the cloud forest. Cal, responding to her phrasing, nodded in reply. Rather than questioning her, they assumed she had a good reason and continued to enjoy the quiet reprieve in the midst of the mist.

After a few minutes the couple on the bench whom Lydia had observed earlier got up and started back down the path. A minute later a mild breeze pushed just enough of the cloud off the lake for them to catch a glimpse, then it was gone again.

Quietly, Lydia got up, motioned to the others to head toward the path continuing on up. Questions on their faces, they followed her. "I think the couple that left may be our spies for the day," she said quietly. "I suggest the gentlemen go first up the path, then Gretchen and Ben, and I'll bring up the rear with Jaime. I don't think there will be a problem, but this way we can look out for each other."

Everyone except Gretchen and Ben nodded at Lydia's plan, but they complied with the arrangement.

The climb up went slowly, with Gretchen and Ben stopping to admire the foliage and occasional animals and to take pictures. The others were tolerant of the slow progress, partly because they suspected that the two needed to occasionally catch their breath.

When the grade of the road started to descend, Jesus motioned the group together. "It looks very foggy ahead," he said. "I think we need to review what to do if we cannot see each other." Others nodded. "The path goes down from here and comes out on the pavement right above the museum. We just keep moving forward and meet at the museum if we don't see someone before then."

"Sounds good," said Calvin, "But shouldn't we call out if we have a problem?"

"Only if you have a problem," replied Lydia and Jesus in unison. They chuckled softly.

"We don't want to advertize our location just in case we still have a tail," replied Jesus. "However, these people are not today acting like they want to hurt us."

"Not yet," responded Lydia. "I think they are trying to figure us out."

Jesus and Cal move out first, with Lydia and Jaime sandwiching the Parks. As Jesus had predicted, the cloud thickened until the sides of the path could barely be seen. Each couple continued to walk, talking quietly with each other, not worried about the fact that they could no longer see the whole group.

However, the path continued longer than anyone remembered, and Cal became concerned. "Let's stop and let Mom and Dad catch up to us," he suggested to Jesus. Jesus promptly agreed. They stepped off to the side of the path to make room for those behind them. It was now so foggy that they could not see across the trail.

Soon Calvin and Jesus heard voices. They quickly realized that the voices were not from Gretchen and Ben, and both instinctively drew further off the path. A few large leaves fell in front of them as they moved, forming a partial screen between them and anyone on the trail. They stood very still.

"Do you think they are ahead of us or behind us?" asked a female voice in Spanish.

The response, by a man, was also in Spanish. "I have no way of knowing. When cutting through a jungle it is hard to keep a sense of direction."

"Why are we following them anyway?"

"Because Don Lupe told us to. That is all I know."

"They do not seem like people who would double cross him in a deal."

"Unless they are police of some kind."

"The older couple? Police?"

They moved on down the trail; their voices, as well as their bodies, lost in the mist.

Calvin and Jesus looked at each other and then back at the trail. More voices were heard.

"The mist is good for my skin, I think," Gretchen was heard to say. "But I wish we could see the beautiful plants as we walked."

"It spooks me a little," said Jaime. "Someone could jump out right in front of us..."

Jesus spoke softly but distinctly to Cal. "I think it is best to declare ourselves now."

There was a slight start from Ben, and Lydia swung herself between the Parks and the voice. "Jesus?" she asked.

"*Sí, señorita.*"

"And Calvin too," replied the younger Parks family member.

"We were too far ahead, so we decided to wait for the rest of you." continued Jesus.

"Good idea," replied Lydia.

"And we learned something," said Cal.

"What?"

"The couple who has been following us does not know why they are doing it."

Jesus continued, "They are following us because someone named Don Lupe told them to."

"Don Lupe," muttered Jaime.

"How do you know this?" asked Lydia.

"The couple had cut through the jungle trying to find us and were talking quietly together. They did not see us."

"Good. Then they don't know what they've told us."

"What do we do when we get down to the bottom?" asked Gretchen.

Lydia and Jesus and Jaime looked at each other.

"It depends somewhat on what happens at the bottom," said Jaime.

Lydia nodded. "I don't think we want to act like something is wrong."

Jesus added, "A little time in the gift shop and museum should be doable, if all is quiet below."

Gretchen smiled.

At the bottom of the path, all was quiet, except for the low happy chattering of the Parks' group.

"What's next, *señora*?" asked Jesus.

"*El baño, señor,*" said Gretchen, heading for the little sign with the woman on it. Lydia followed. When they came out, Cal offered his mom a bottled water which she gratefully took.

They sat in chairs outside while they sipped their water and recovered from their hike. By the time she was done, Gretchen had spotted some items in the window of the gift shop she wanted to investigate. Ben and Cal headed for the museum with Jesus following along. Jaime and Lydia followed Gretchen into the shop.

Half an hour later the museum group joined the rest in the gift shop. Gretchen was making her final decisions and a few minutes later stood in the checkout line. As she waited, trying to figure out the conversion rate of *colones* to dollars, a couple got in line behind her. They were chatting as they approached, and she noticed Cal's expression tighten slightly. This told her who the couple were.

"Oh, you got an unusual one!" exclaimed the lady behind her in perfect English. "I love those wooden puzzle boxes."

CHAPTER 7

Gretchen, a little flustered, said, "Thank you." She turned her head enough to get a glimpse of the man behind the lady, but he was looking past her at Jesus.

"I have never seen a puzzle box in the shape of a sea turtle," continued the woman, crowding a little closer.

Gretchen stepped back. "Honey," she drawled out the word with a decidedly Southern flare. "I don't know what it's like where you come from, but where I come from strangers remain at a distance when they speak to you."

The woman remained motionless.

Gretchen continued. "Crowding ..." Gretchen stepped back one more step, "... is considered very rude," Gretchen raised an eyebrow and gave the woman her teacher look, "and maybe the sign of a pickpocket."

"Pickpocket?" The woman looked puzzled.

The man behind her leaned in and murmured a word in Spanish.

"Oh!" said the woman and moved quickly backwards.

Gretchen, clasping her purse tightly and keeping her eyebrow raised, she turned to the cashier. The cashier motioned the couple further back. Gretchen only opened her purse when the couple had moved back about ten feet. She paid the clerk and then, while waiting for change, took out her ipod and snapped a photo of them. While they watched, with mouths open, she hit send and the photo was sent to destination unknown.

The man cursed under his breath, snatched the tourist trinkets out of the woman's hands, threw them on the counter, and pulled her out of the store.

Lydia watched the man pull out his phone and hold it to his ear. She watched him take the phone away from his ear, look at it, and then put it away. The couple continued to argue as they headed toward their car. Lydia saw them get in a brown car before she turned back to the group. "Did that photo actually go somewhere?" she asked Gretchen.

"Don't think so," replied Gretchen. "I don't think they have WIFI up here yet. But I did get the photo."

"I think mine went," Ben stated. "Got a photo in the middle of Gretchen's crowding routine. Sent it to you and to the American Embassy. Don't know what kind of data plan you have on this phone, but I didn't want to ask and call attention to myself."

Lydia dropped her jaw in amazement. She wanted to ask, "Are you sure you've never done any work for the CIA before?" but didn't dare in front of the store clerk.

Gretchen gathered up her purchases and was ready to move on. "What next?"

Jaime answered, "Lunch at one of the restaurants we passed coming up."

"One with hummingbirds," suggested Cal.

Jaime drove to a low-roofed building hanging over the side of the mountain. After ordering traditional Costa Rican fare, Gretchen got up and walked over to the door leading to a narrow balcony. She stood there looking over the lush scene below. Then, suddenly there was a quick, bee-like movement and a shimmering green hummingbird paused next to a hanging bowl of sugar water. It hung there in the air for three seconds; and then, in another sudden movement, it was gone. Gretchen opened the door and stepped through. She stood very still just outside the door. Again and again the tiny birds came – golden, ruby, and emerald living jewels – totally ignoring the quiet woman while sipping their nectar lunches.

There was a gentle tap on the glass door behind

Gretchen. Turning, Gretchen met her husband's smiling face just a couple feet away on the other side of the glass. He lifted a hand positioned like he was holding a sandwich to his mouth. Gretchen recognized the sign for "eat" and nodded. Her hand on the door handle, she turned to watch one more feathered ruby before re-entering the restaurant.

Later, back in the van, the group talked about their plans. "I know that I said, 'Arenal,'" Lydia explained, "but I think it is best to change it up."

Jesus looked at the Parks and asked, "Have you seen Cartago? The cathedral?" Ben and Gretchen shook their heads in the negative. Jesus looked at Lydia. "It's not too far from the capital. With the Park's interest in things religious, it could be a nice stop. And Don Lupe's locals would hesitate doing anything in this Catholic holy site."

Jaime spoke. "I know of a place not too far away where they could spend the night. Beautiful. Hot spring-fed baths. A little off the usual tourist route, but not too isolated."

Lydia made a call. After a few minutes, she nodded. "Head toward Cartago, Jaime. Our luggage goes ahead of us."

They navigated the *barrios* around the North and East side of San José, finally arriving in Cartago, the spiritual capital of Costa Rica. First stop was the ruins of the old cathedral, now more of a city park with flowers planted inside the ruins themselves. Calvin talked about his last experience at that site.

"I read in the paper that the Good Friday procession would start at 9 a.m. and decided that, to understand the country that I'm living in, it would be good to experience. So, I took an early bus, arriving in town about 8:15 a.m. I was surprised that there was no one in the center of town. I looked around the cathedral square and walked down to this ruin. It seemed that I should leave the square to the Catholic faithful, so I settled on staying in this ruin's park.

"Across the street, somber music was playing. Roving merchants positioned themselves to sell *paraguas* – umbrellas for either the sun or rain -- religious trinkets, and *helados* and shaved ice *con dos leches* – snow cones with sweetened condensed milk and powdered milk.

"The music continued, people slowly arrived, and the merchants began to do a good business as the sun grew hotter. Finally, at about 11:00 a.m., I could see the procession a few blocks down. By that time I had figured out that the procession had started somewhere away from Cartago's center and was making its way very slowly toward the basilica. It took another hour to make it to the block containing the ruins. First came some priests, then Roman soldiers marched. Step. Pause. Step. Pause. Then a float, I guess that is what you would call it, came bearing a large statue of Christ carrying the cross. When it had passed, I figured it was time for me to leave."

Gretchen looked pleased. "Thank you, Calvin, for sharing your impressions. It makes what I am seeing more meaningful."

Jesus added, "It is interesting to hear the impressions of an outsider. It is so much of our culture that we do not question it."

Jaime started ushering the group back to the car. "Wait until you get to experience the *Dia de Los Angeles*."

"Yes," said Cal. "I couldn't believe the television reports about people walking on their knees from the edge of town to the Cathedral's altar."

The new cathedral shown in the sunshine. Gretchen gasped at her first sight of the magnificent edifice.

Jesus got out first and walked over to a car parked nearby. "A few minutes, please." he said to the driver inside, and walked toward the front entrance of the building. The rest took their time getting to the door.

As they approached the entrance, they saw Jesus cross himself and leave a pew close to the front of the room.

He turned, smiling at the group, and said as he passed them, "Now I am ready to see if the arrested maids are also my attackers."

"*Vaya con Dios*," Ben said as Jesus passed.

"Cartago was founded by Spanish explorer Coronado and was the first capital of Costa Rica." Jaime took over the duties of tour guide. "This building was built after a major eruption of volcano Irazu, which is not far from here. Much of Cartago was destroyed at that time.

"What makes Cartago still the religious capital of Costa Rica deals with a very old story. The Virgin Mary appeared to a young girl in the form of a small, black statue. There are more details to the story, but the conclusion is that the church was built on the site of the girl's vision and *La Negrita*, the small black statue, is in that special case in front of the crucifix."

"May we sit for a while, here at the back, and pray?" asked Gretchen.

"Are you Catholic, ma'am?"

"No, but the same Jesus we worship is illustrated in the art work of this place. We would like to take time to pray," said Ben.

"Most certainly," replied Jaime.

Jaime and Lydia retreated to a position by the door while Gretchen and Ben prayed. They did not hear the words spoken, but saw the peaceful expression on the couple as they arose. Cal sat in quiet contemplation not far from his parents, but he did not attempt to join them.

"Time to go?" Lydia's words were not in the form of a question, but her tone was.

"Yes," said the three Parks together.

Narrow winding roads brought them to a well protected traditionally barred entrance to a resort built into the hillside. They parked their vehicle inside the bars, and walked toward the entrance. Jaime did the talking and soon they were entering a pretty villa with a common area between several bedrooms. The suitcases were already parked in the main room.

Gretchen rolled her suitcase into the nearest bedroom and collapsed onto the bed. She closed her eyes. Lydia walked in and asked, "Are you all right?"

Gretchen nodded without opening her eyes. "I'm not really that tired. It's just been the tension of the day."

"You can rest," replied Lydia. "We are going to wait for Jesus' return before we go to supper. He is supposed to bring the appropriate dressware."

""Dressware?"

"Whatever you call it when you have to dress formally for dinner."

Gretchen's eyebrows went up. "Fancy place?"

"In some ways. I think you'll like the hot tubs."

Gretchen smiled, still not opening her eyes. Lydia left her in peace.

About an hour and a half later, Jesus walked through the door, his arms loaded with garment bags. He handed two sparkly long gowns to Lydia, who promptly took one into Gretchen who was just waking up. While the men slipped into rented tuxes, Gretchen and Lydia slipped into the silky gowns with loose flowing lines which would adapt to multiple sizes of women. Lydia cinched hers in at the waist with a belt, but Gretchen chose to let the drapes hide some of her middle-aged bulges.

Ben whistled at Gretchen as she came out in the silver gown which complemented her gray hair and pinkish complexion. Not to be out-done, Jesus and Calvin whistled when Lydia joined her. She did look nice as the yellow and golden dress floated around her.

Ben offered an arm to Gretchen and Jesus did the same for Lydia. Cal led the way to the dining hall while Jaime brought up the rear. They found themselves in a large room lit with candelabra and already full of delightful smells. Jaime had already ordered, so wonderful salads containing a wide variety of fruits and vegetables were served immediately. Rice and beans followed, of course, accompanied by platters of fish, chicken, and pork. All were delicately seasoned with cilantro, garlic, lime, and other spices. Fruit smoothies accompanied this, and the meal was topped off with *arróz con leche*, *tres leches* cake, and small chocolate candies.

While they ate, each of them found themselves trying to casually observe their fellow diners. As per the requirements of the dining room, all were formally dressed. Most spoke in Spanish, but there were a couple of other English-speaking tables. One was a family obviously on vacation, and the other looked like a group of businessmen. Of the Spanish-speaking tables, there were a variety of ages and people-groups represented. None of them appeared to be interested in the Parks' table. Even Lydia relaxed some as the meal progressed, though all remained alert.

As they started back toward their house, the kitchen was wheeling out a series of carts loaded with food. Jesus and Ben held the doors open for the carts to go through. The waiters who pushed the carts chattered to each other excitedly in Spanish. Lydia couldn't follow the fast conversation, but she noticed Jesus stiffen at one point.

Back in their own villa, Lydia asked, "What was that all about?"

Cal spoke first. "I caught this much - that taking food to the room was unusual here."

"*Sí*," said Jesus, "it is. But what caught my attention was someone they referred to simply as the don."

"I noticed that, too," said Jaime. "It couldn't be Don Lupe could it? Don is just a title of respect."

Jesus shrugged. "Probably not our guy, but it did give me a start."

Gretchen sighed.

Lydia glanced her way and said, "Someone eating this late will probably not be up early. We can enjoy the spa and pool in the morning and keep an eye open for a possible move later in the day." She walked toward the room phone. "I'm going to call housekeeping and ask that our laundry be done overnight."

"Good idea," said Ben with a dead-pan face. "I like to have nice clean clothes while I'm on the run."

Cal snorted. He knew his dad's sense of humor. Then he turned to Jesus. "By the way, can you talk about your police experience this afternoon?"

Jesus summarized very briefly. "I was able to identify the two more easily than I had imagined. They are still in custody."

The conversation turned from serious things to more tourist-like chatter. "Dad, Mom, we were close to this place last year during your visit."

"We were?" asked Gretchen.

"Yup, the Lancaster Gardens are not far from here."

"Oh, I loved that place," she said.

"Me too," added Ben.

"Have you been to Volcano Irazu?" asked Jaime.

The Parks all shook their heads.

There was a knock on the door, and all scurried to gather their dirty clothes for the maid. When she had left, Jaime continued. "May I suggest a late morning outing to this volcano. It is the highest spot in Costa Rica, and on a clear day you can see both coasts of Costa Rica – the Pacific and Atlantic."

Conversation on the merits of various Costa Rican sites continued until they caught each other yawning. Showers and comfortable beds would finish their day. Lydia suggested that before each went to sleep, they open their door a crack so that any unusual sounds could reach all.

Calvin began to chuckle. Ben got red in the face. Gretchen whispered to him, "Snoring is not an unusual sound. No one will care."

"One more thing," added Jesus, "*Señora y señor*, do you plan to pray before you sleep?

CHAPTER 8

"Yes." Ben nodded.

"Well then, may I join you?" asked Jesus.

"Certainly," Ben replied.

"And me, Dad?" This from Cal.

As the four moved the chairs they were sitting in closer together, Lydia looked uncomfortably at Jaime. He motioned to her and moved to join the group, saying softly, "It will not hurt, *Señorita*." Lydia hesitated a moment and then moved to join the group.

Ben assured everyone that joining their circle did not mean that they had to pray out loud. "And there are no special words we expect when we pray – no *Thees* or *Thous*, anything like that." Ben and Gretchen folded their hands. Jesus crossed himself and bowed. Cal left his hands open, held palms up. Jaime hesitated a moment and crossed himself also. Lydia bowed her head, but left her eyes open.

Ben was the first to speak. "God, you have been leading us into some big adventures these last couple of days." He paused.

Gretchen continued, "Thanks for keeping us safe through those adventures."

"Especially me," added Jesus. "I was so scared that night, but the blow on my head has healed very quickly. *Muchas gracias, Señor.*"

There was a time of silence. Then Jaime said, "*Dios me da la Sernidad para aceptar las cosas que no puedo cambiar, el Corage para cambiar las que sí puedo y la Sabidura para reconocer la diferencia.*"

Calvin added, "Yes, Lord, we need your peace to do

our best in this unusual situation. Help us to communicate well with each other and be alert to what we need to see and react to."

After another short silence, the amen came from Lydia. They all retired quietly to their rooms and their beds. Even Lydia slept soundly until about 5:30 in the morning.

At that time on Friday morning, she was awakened by a rap on the door. Standing before her eyes were open, Lydia moved quietly to the door. She peeked out the window, but saw no one outside. Glancing down, she saw a package left on the stoop. Cautiously, she opened the door and checked out the bundle. It contained clean, folded clothes. Lydia smiled; they had done the laundry quickly. That was a big help. She pulled the bundle inside.

Behind it she noticed something else. Again on the alert, Lydia straightened up. Approaching from behind was Gretchen and Cal.

Lydia pointed to the bundle. "Clean clothes," she whispered.

Gretchen pointed toward the bedroom she'd just left. "Snoring." she whispered.

Calvin pointed toward the room he'd shared with the other two young men. He repeated his mother's one word statement. "Snoring."

Lydia smiled, but it was a tight smile. She pointed to the other things left on the stoop. Gretchen and Cal leaned forward to look. A silver platter contained a covered glass dish of tropical fruit salad, a loaf of warm bread wrapped in a towel which did not keep in the delicious aroma, and a bottle of some kind of beverage. A small card sat next to the fruit dish.

"Did anyone order this?" asked Lydia. Calvin and Gretchen shook their heads. "I think the others would have said something, don't you?" Both nodded. She bent to pick up the card. What she read brought a puzzled look to her face:

"We regret the inconvenience, Don Philip. Please accept with our compliments."

"Another Don," muttered Ben, scratching his head and yawning as he wandered out of his room.

"Probably would call you Don Benjamin, if they were writing a similar note," responded Jaime who had obviously slept in his clothes.

Jesus followed quietly behind him. "Don Lupe ... Don Philip ..."

Gretchen was exploring the clothes package. She held up a man's dress shirt with a perfectly starched collar much larger than any of the men in their party.

Cal's eyebrows went up. He reached down and picked up a slinky red something and blushed. He glanced at Lydia who also blushed and shook her head. He couldn't bring himself to look at his mother.

Gretchen chuckled. "Even if that thing is supposed to fit snuggly, I could never squeeze into it."

Lydia reached for the suite's phone. She dialed the front desk while Cal reached for the one item no one had noticed outside the room before: a newspaper. He walked over to a comfortable chair and sat down, opening up the latest edition of the Costa Rican paper *La Nación*.

After trying to communicate with the night clerk who wasn't fluent in English, Lydia passed the phone to Jesus. All except Calvin listened in on the conversation with various degrees of understanding because of various levels of Spanish literacy. Calvin studied the front page of the paper with unusual intensity.

Shortly after Jesus hung up, a flustered maid came to

the door followed by a sleepy-looking young male manager. The maid apologized in Spanish, and gathered the clothing, leaving a similar package in its place. Then she took the tray and its contents out to a cart. The manager apologized in English and let them know that such food and more would be available at the breakfast buffet in a very few minutes.

As they were about to leave, Calvin called out, "You forgot the newspaper."

"Oh, no, *señor*," replied the manager. "*Every* guest gets *La Nación*!" Bowing, he backed out of the room.

Lydia sunk into the couch. "I am so glad it was their mistake!" she exclaimed. " I was hoping it wasn't some kind of trick with poisoned food."

The rest also found seats. Gretchen and Jaime frowned. Ben drummed his fingers on his leg.

Jesus responded to Calvin pointing to a particular spot in the paper and read where he pointed. "Very interesting, Calvin," said Jesus. He turned toward the rest. "It seems that there are articles both about Don Lupe and an U.S. man named Philip."

"Probably have no connection." mumbled Gretchen.

"Let's see what the articles say, before we decide that," Lydia replied.

"You're right." Gretchen nodded.

Jesus started translating the text of one of the articles. "Chicago business man Philip Camron is in Costa Rica to investigate the possibility of forming new business opportunities in our country with local partners." Jesus continued by summarizing what followed. "It names several local entrepreneurs and other international connections ... and the caption in the picture above the article says that 'Camron is shown here sitting next to Lupe Mora Alba of Columbia at the National Theater.'"

Eyebrows shot up in surprise.

"It's possible that the seating arrangement is accidental," commented Jaime.

"Possible," said Lydia in a doubtful tone.

"Doubtful," added Calvin. "*I* know that Mora is the name of a drug cartel family. If *I* know it, then certainly Mr. Camron's people should know it. I think the paper was trying to tell us more than it could safely say in words."

"Lydia, if the CIA needs another operative, this young man might be a good one." This from Jesus.

"No way!" exclaimed Calvin, "And I'd rather you not ask my parents, either."

Lydia smiled wryly. "It was no one's intention to get them so deeply involved, but ..." she paused for a moment, "I still think they were a good choice."

Jesus and Jaime took the paper back to their room to study. After a while, they asked for Ben's phone, which they figured was the most secure, and spent some time talking to someone on it. The rest took their clean clothes, put them away and finished getting ready for the day. By the time all had finished these chores, Jesus walked out, clapped his hands together in front of him, and said, "Are we ready for breakfast?"

"Sure," replied Ben, and Calvin snapped on his money belt.

They walked up the hill to the same building where they had eaten the night before and found a beautiful breakfast buffet. After eating their fill, Lydia suggested that they pack up, except for their swimsuits and take advantage of the outdoor hot tubs before making final plans for the day.

They changed, wrapped themselves in thick robes found in the room, and walked through the cool morning air toward a series of small shelters.

Jaime explained, "The higher up the mountain you go, the hotter the water in your tub. There are two tubs under each shelter's roof, so two people can relax close together."

Lydia turned to Gretchen, "You and Ben could take one shelter, if you would like."

Gretchen blushed a little. "Ben likes hotter water than I do. I think he and Cal are going to hike up a ways together to see how hot they can stand it. Are you a hot water person?"

Lydia smiled. This solved a small security concern. "I have no desire to scorch myself. I'll stay with you."

Jaime hiked up the mountain with Ben and Calvin. Jesus dropped back below the ladies. Gretchen turned her attention to the third shelter up the mountain path. Old cast iron tubs were sunk into wooden platforms. Corroded metal faucets attested to the warmth and the mineral content in the water filling the tubs. Surrounded by lush tropical vegetation, it made for a peaceful and quaint setting.

Gretchen eased into a tub. The warmth immediately began to relieve tension from muscles stressed by the unaccustomed activities of the last few days. She leaned her head against the back of the tub and breathed deeply. After a few minutes she turned her head toward Lydia.

Lydia was in a similar position, but she had kept her eyes open.

"Heavenly," commented Gretchen.

"I agree," replied Lydia. "I wish life had more of these moments."

Gretchen sighed. "That would take a whole lot more people being a whole lot more interested in heaven, I think."

Lydia pivoted her head toward Gretchen. "You mean getting converted?" she asked, almost biting her lip for saying so. She had certainly provided the perfect opening for one of those religious talks.

Gretchen snorted. "Kind of. Converted back, more like it." She paused, but Lydia was quiet. "Changed back into what they were made to be in the beginning."

"So you think everyone was made good, and it's downhill from there?" Lydia bit her lip again.

"What God made was good, and that includes people, I think," replied Gretchen. "It does seem that when we try to improve our lives without Divine assistance, we do just the opposite."

Lydia smiled. She agreed with Gretchen, basically; but she was hoping that this was the end of the religion stuff.

They both lay in their personal tubs, soaking up the atmosphere and listening to the intermittent murmurs of their companions. No one else seemed to be awake yet, at least there was no one uphill from the dining hall. The whole world seemed at peace, except in Lydia's mind. Gretchen was letting the conversation drop, but Lydia couldn't contain her curiosity. What kind of relationship with God did Gretchen think would – could – really change people for the better? It would sure make her job a lot easier.

"What kind of relationship with God do you think would make any real difference in people?" Lydia couldn't believe that she was the one starting the conversation up again.

"Well," Gretchen began slowly. Lydia didn't know that the slowness was caused by the silent prayer for guidance Gretchen sent up. "I think the first quality of a life-changing relationship with God is admitting that you need His help ... that there are some things in this life you can't do without divine assistance."

"That makes sense," responded Lydia, "assuming, that is, you believe God would stoop to helping us poor humans."

Gretchen chuckled. "Please forgive me if I sound critical," she said. "You're not saying anything that I haven't heard before. It's just that … Well, if you needed my help, it would depend more upon whether *I* was willing to help than it would whether *you thought* I was willing to help."

"Huh?"

"If I was willing to help, you might get some help even if you didn't expect me to do anything."

"That's true," responded Lydia. "Of course if you didn't know and I didn't ask…"

"Exactly." Gretchen nodded. "It does still make a difference whether we believe God wants to help us, just not in the way we usually think."

"So God can't help if we don't tell him we need help?" Lydia was surprised to hear Gretchen say something that made her God sound so powerless.

"Oh, I believe God knows and can help, but he often follows a policy of not interfering unless He is wanted."

"Good for Him – or Her," replied Lydia, hoping to throw Gretchen off track.

"We need a different pronoun for God, don't we?" responded Gretchen. "Something unique for the One who created male and female, but isn't just one or the other."

Lydia made a noise of consent.

"But God does interfere sometimes even when He's not asked," continued Gretchen.

Lydia realized that she had not thrown her off track.

"The whole business of Jesus coming to earth was an attempt to reach people who didn't know how badly they needed to be helped."

"And Buddha and Confucius, and the Dali Lama?" Lydia was pretty sure she knew how Gretchen would feel about this, but she was feeling a little ornery herself.

"You know, Buddha didn't really talk about God and heaven and that kind of thing," said Gretchen thoughtfully. "He had a lot of good things to say about this life."

Lydia looked at Gretchen in surprise.

"I don't know that much about Confucius. I think he's one of those people who gets credit for a lot more than he actually said or did. Like Shakespeare or that football coach everyone is always quoting."

Lydia smiled.

"I went to the Dali Lama's website once … Maybe I'm too western in my thinking to get my head around what he says."

"Does that mean you think he's from God or not?" Lydia cut to the chase.

"Not like Jesus," replied Gretchen. Again she was doing her best to keep from being distracted by a side issue. "Jesus came to show God's love, power, and desire to redeem fallen humanity. I can't think of anyone else who has lived on this earth and so clearly had that purpose."

"So, I've got to accept Jesus as my Savior to get to heaven, right?" Lydia was gazing sharply at Gretchen now.

Gretchen chuckled again. "Interesting that you think that," she replied.

"I don't …" Lydia stopped, realizing what Gretchen was doing.

"Because that's what Jesus himself said."

Lydia couldn't remember the exact verse, but she remembered something from Sunday School which started "I am the Way…" She kept quiet, realizing that this whole conversation was her fault.

Gretchen sat up. She looked at Lydia. "Have you?" she asked.

"Have I?" Lydia thought for a moment as Gretchen remained silent. She knew what Gretchen was asking. "Yes, I have had enough of this tub, no matter how delightful. Would you like to go for a swim?"

CHAPTER 9

Only about nine a.m. on Friday, it was still cool enough that they chose the warm water pool. The men of their party joined them within a few minutes. They spent a half hour swimming, went back to the room to change, and then had a meeting in the main room. Jaime had changed quickly and left the apartment some time before anyone else was finished dressing. As the discussion turned to the plans for the day, Jaime came in carrying two large baskets. He held them up a little, saying simply, "Lunch."

"Irazu?" asked Calvin.

Jaime nodded. "Yes. And I've been using Ben's phone. I just got a callback on the story we read in the paper. I suggest that you take your things with you and explore another beautiful corner of Costa Rica this evening."

"What did you learn?" asked Lydia.

"It appears that a meeting of a variety of businessmen from several countries is taking place here today."

There was silence in the room.

"I am going to ask Jesus and or Calvin to drive today. I plan to stay here and will be joined by several others who would like to spend some time in a hot tub."

Gretchen and Ben looked serious. Gretchen put a hand on Jaime's arm. "Be safe," she said.

"We will be praying for you," added Ben.

"*Gracias, señor.*"

Lydia noticed in the rear-view mirror that Gretchen

and Ben had their heads bowed as they started back down the narrow road toward Cartago. Somehow those prayers helped even her feel better about leaving Jaime behind.

They passed through Cartago again and started on the road to the highest point in Costa Rica. All were wondering if it would be clear enough to see both the Atlantic and Pacific from the top of Irazu. The morning was still hazy, so it was doubtful that they would get that view. However, all hoped that they would rise above the clouds.

The road became narrower, winding, and steep. The mist of the morning seemed now tinged with an acrid smell. Suddenly the van rumbled over what seemed like a particularly rough patch of road. A few rocks rolled down the hillside across the road.

"What was that?" asked Ben.

Jesus looked stern.

Lydia asked, "Was that an earthquake?"

Jesus nodded. "And since we are on the side of a volcano, *Señorita*, it may be associated with volcanic activity."

"Like an eruption?" asked Gretchen.

"The last noticeable activity was about 20 years ago," Jesus explained. "Ash, mudslides, and rocks like these, moving around."

"Oh."

"What is your recommendation?" asked Lydia.

"Well, miss, I do not think this is the day to have a picnic on this mountain. I think it would be best to turn around and discuss an alternative destination."

Gretchen exhaled deeply. "I agree."

Calvin pouted. "Spoilsports. I've always wanted to be in the midst of a volcanic eruption." Eyeing his mother, he went on. "Ash clouds, landslides, lava sailing through the sky…"

"Irazu is not known for the lava, Cal," Jesus replied.

"Cal's just trying to get my goat," Gretchen told him.

"Your goat? Oh! an idiom." Jesus nodded as he finished maneuvering a U-turn with the van on the narrow road.

They discussed various options as they descended the volcano, and there was one more minor tremor confirming for them that they had made the right choice in turning around. Lydia turned on the radio and they listened to a reporter announce that Irazu Park would be closed for the rest of that day and that people might want to get dust masks or wet cloths ready in case of an ash release. No definite decisions had been made, but Jesus drove west toward the capital of San José.

Cal finally said, "I wanted to take my folks to a beach sometime during their stay here – a different one – but my knowledge of beaches is somewhat limited."

"I know one," replied Jesus. "Not an international tourist beach, but one more for locals. We can arrive unannounced. It is not the most famous, but it is very nice, relatively quiet, and more the real Costa Rica."

"It sounds perfect," said Ben.

Lydia got on the phone, and, after a few minutes of discussion between herself, some official, and Jesus, it was decided that their destination would be Jesus' beach. By this time they were passing Terra Mall in Tres Rios east of San José. Gretchen glanced at the inviting shopping destination and asked, "Do they have restrooms in the mall?"

Ben and Cal laughed.

Jesus smiled. "We have passed the exit for the mall, but I could go back…"

Cal interrupted, "Not too far ahead is another shopping place you would like, Mom." He turned toward Jesus.

"Mom is a great Walmart shopper back home."

"Do they have Walmarts in Costa Rica?" Gretchen asked with an eager note in her voice.

"Yes, Mom, there was a department store here already, but Walmart has taken it over."

Jesus made a strange noise in his throat. "Maybe Walmart will do what William Walker could not."

Cal added, "And McDonald's and KFC and Burger King."

Gretchen and Ben looked puzzled.

Jesus gave them a brief history lesson. "Walker, a U.S. southerner, conceived the idea of conquering Central American countries and bringing them into the United States as slave states, tipping the balance of power in your country on that issue. We celebrate his defeat in Costa Rica on Juan Santamaria Day."

They turned at the next exit, entered the store's parking lot, took a ticket from the lot's attendant, and found a spot to park. On the way into the store, both Lydia and Ben stopped and got more cash from the Red ATH (ATM) outside the store. Passing through the entryway checkpoint, Gretchen turned toward the restrooms, followed by Lydia. Coming out, she got out a piece of paper from her purse and started writing a list of things to look for in the store.

It was obvious that Gretchen and Ben enjoyed the store. They went up and down every isle and found several things of interest to them. Ben got several Costa Rican traditional coffee makers (a mesh stretched around a looped wire) and a pad of paper and a new pen. Gretchen found another blouse, a scarf, and some suntan lotion. Cal picked up the latest copy of the English-language paper *The Tico Times* for his dad. Jesus found a book to read. Lydia even found a shawl she liked.

When they got to the grocery section, Gretchen had to examine every exotic fruit and compare prices with those in the States. Everyone was hungry by the time they got to the in-store lunch buffet, so it was decided that they would eat before they left the store.

"What about Jaime's picnic baskets?" asked Gretchen.

Jesus had already been thinking about that. "On our way through town I think I can find someone who would be blessed by them."

Everyone except Ben had rice and beans as part of their meal. Ben went for bread and beef. Gretchen tried the tamales and was surprised to find out how bland they tasted. Lydia picked a plate full of fruit for them to share.

While they were eating Ben returned to the conversation they had had earlier. "Why is your patriotic holiday called Juan Santamaria Day?"

Calvin answered, "Santamaria was a drummer boy for the combined Central American army in the war against William Walker. He managed to set fire to the building that Walker's army was using for their stronghold. This turned the tide of the battle."

After finishing their meal, they checked out, but didn't get past the *Helados* stand without getting *granizados con dos leches* for everyone. These snowcones with sweetened condensed milk and powdered milk poured over the top were the perfect desert for the meal.

Jesus drove on into San José, through busy streets lined with small shops. At one point, he pulled off the main thoroughfare and circled a park. On the far side of the park, he saw a small family huddled around a crippled child close to the road. Jesus hopped out, grabbed the baskets handed him by Ben, and trotted over to the family. "*Para sus familia,*" he said, handing the baskets to the father.

Back inside the van, Jesus explained. "Beggars. It's always hard to determine whether they are really needy or just professionals, but here close to the hospital ..." he nodded toward a large building about a block down a side street, "Often someone in the family is sick."

Ben added, "I checked the baskets before handing them to you, Jesus. Jaime packed everything in ice, so the food is still cool."

Jesus nodded. "Good. We would not want to add to the family's problems." He started to drive back toward the main street.

Suddenly Gretchen leaned forward and strained to look at a spot across the park. "Look! Ben, isn't that Harry Workman over there? See, by that group of young women."

"You mean by the streetwalkers?" asked Jesus.

"Streetwalkers?" Gretchen tried to get another look at the group that she had seen. "I don't know ... I can't tell ... Are you sure they are streetwalkers?"

Jesus shrugged. "I did not get that clear a look. I guess I just assumed that they were by the location and something about their – their movements."

Gretchen faced forward again. "I can't see them anymore. And it probably wasn't him. I didn't see Kitty, and I think they'd be hanging together." She grinned. "I can just see the two of them stopping a prostitute to ask for directions, though. They are pretty naïve; I don't think they have ever been farther from home than the Quad Cities."

Jesus glanced in the rearview window and caught Ben with his eyebrows raised, but neither said anything.

As he turned another corner, Jesus had a sudden thought. Glancing at Lydia, he said, "Lydia, do you think the Parks might like to stop at one of the downtown museums, since we are so close? Would it be permissible?"

Lydia turned toward the Parks. "I think it would. No one knows exactly where we are except the official at the embassy who has Mr. Park's GPS under surveillance. Do you have a preference?"

Gretchen looked at the men in her family. "Well, we went to the Gold Museum last year and it was fantastic. I especially liked the art gallery ... but I'm not sure I feel like being trapped underground this afternoon."

Calvin spoke up. "I never got them to the National History Museum, however."

Jesus turned at the next corner. "The National History Museum it is." He parked in a cramped lot at the bottom of the block containing the museum and noted Gretchen's longing eye as they walked uphill past a covered walkway filled with crafts and tourist items. He leaned close to Lydia and said, "If we have time, we can take the long way back to the van."

Lydia nodded, then frowned. "If someone is following us, the van is about the only way now that they could find us."

Jesus' eyebrows went up. "While you are in the museum, I could fix that." He pointed to the north. "I know where there is a car rental facility."

CHAPTER 10

Lydia nodded again and Jesus turned in his tracks. The rest went on into the museum. Of their reduced party, only Calvin had seen this museum before. Lydia studied the stone spheres, carved by early natives using an unknown process. Ben chuckled over the painted ox carts, imagining a family dressed for church arriving at the front of one of the imposing Catholic edifices in one of these. Gretchen studied the faces in the exhibit of people-groups living in Costa Rica. There were descendents of the native tribes, of African slaves, of Spanish nobility, of Chinese immigrants, and Northern Europeans. "They look just like Americans, only a higher percentage with dark hair."

Jesus murmured softly, "They are Americans, *señora*. Central Americans."

Gretchen blushed. "You caught me, Jesus. They are Americans. The ethnic groups look just like those in the United States, except different percentages of each type."

But it was when they went downstairs that Gretchen was totally overwhelmed.

"Great!" exclaimed Calvin. "The temporary butterfly exhibit is open again!"

They passed through a screened door into a large open area, covered by some kind of netting. Exotic plants made a garden with paved walkways circling through them. Through the air flew bright flashes of color: red, yellow, black and white striped. The largest of these flashes were a stunning blue from the Blue Morpho butterflies.

"Oh, how beautiful!" exclaimed Gretchen, "but where do they go? I cannot see any that are still – that have landed."

Jesus smiled as Calvin led his mother toward a bowl of rotting fruit. Around the bowl were brownish gray butterflies about the same size as the brilliant blue ones. The only thing interesting about these butterflies were the large eyespots on the dull wings. As Gretchen got close, one took off. When the large gray wings opened, iridescent blue appeared. "Oh," was all that Gretchen could manage to say.

It took them over half an hour to drag Gretchen out of the butterfly garden, though no one was trying too hard to get her to leave. There was something fascinating about the living jewels. It was especially thrilling to have one light on you, if you stood or sat very still in their midst.

As they left the museum, they found Jesus lounging outside. He nodded and joined them as they walked back down the street. Moving close to Lydia, he said, "The embassy has been called to pick up their van." Lydia nodded, then forgot about Jesus' errand as she found herself bartering with some of the craft merchants for their wares.

Everyone knew that, being "on-the-run," they could not buy any large items, but skirts, T-shirts, and small items made from wood and shells didn't take up much room. They could even replace some of the clothes they had brought from home with these colorful purchases, if they so desired. It did not take more than another half hour (though Gretchen knew she could have easily spent the rest of the day there) for everyone to be ready to return to their vehicle.

A puzzled look appeared on most of their faces when the van they had been riding in was not where they had left it. However, light dawned as they remembered Jesus' errand. He guided them to a small SUV, just the right size for five people with luggage. Luggage was already piled in the back; they added their purchases to it, and found their seats.

Jesus again got into the driver's seat and took off. As he drove, he said, "When I was a child, we would sometimes take the bus in the morning to Puntarenas Beach and stay until the time of the bus in the afternoon." He drove past the bus terminal on his way to the highway that wound through mountains toward the Pacific Ocean. In self-defense, Gretchen and Ben decided that they would nap for most of the journey. Watching the oncoming traffic and the drop-away cliff was not conducive to their feelings of safety. Asleep, the two hour trip passed quickly.

The couple was just awakening as Jesus stopped in front of a small hotel. He hoped out and went inside. Coming out a few moments later, he shook his head. "But the manager called to another place. There is 'no room in the inn;' however, the owner of the next hotel also has a rental house which happens to be empty because of the illness of the usual summer occupant." He grinned. "Three bedrooms. Two baths. Let's go look!"

Fifteen minutes later Jesus was shaking another innkeeper's hand and Gretchen and Ben were strolling under the shade of the trees surrounding the little bungalow which stood on a quiet street just half a block from the beach. The main room's window was set at an angle so that it gave the best view of the ocean. Lydia looked around at the other houses in the neighborhood. They had been told that most were rented by the week or by the month to tourists. The home directly across the street was still occupied by an elderly woman who had not wanted to sell. Every home contained barred windows, but this area was considered safe enough that the high metal fences with spikes at the top, found everywhere in the Central Valley, were absent here.

Jesus walked toward her. "*Señorita*, I have told a lie in the line of work."

"In the line of work?"

"*Sí*. I said that you were my girlfriend and the rest were your family, down here to meet me."

"Oh!"

"Lydia, I do not intend to take advantage of this lie, but I should probably address you less formally."

"Of course." Lydia tried to analyze her feelings about this, but failed.

"*Lo siento* – I'm sorry, Lydia."

"Oh, no! It makes perfect sense. It is the most likely story, actually." Lydia forced a smile and reached out to touch Jesus' hand for a moment.

Jesus turned that hand and squeezed Lydia's. Letting it go and stepping back, he said, "*Gracias*. I think once we get settled, we can all relax just a little bit. We should be able to stay here more than one night. I paid for the week to go along with my – uh – cover story."

Lydia grinned. "That seems like a reasonable expense. It probably didn't cost more than one night at the fancy tourist places."

"In that you are definitely right ... Lydia."

Everyone except Lydia put things away like they planned to stay a week. Even she put a few things in one of the bathrooms. They found a little open café for an early supper and a small market for breakfast supplies. After putting the things they had purchased in the house's refrigerator, they decided to take a stroll on the beach. The last rays of daylight were fading from the horizon, but the moon and the stars were giving enough light for them to see where they were going.

Little wavelets lapped against the sand. A few small

creatures scurried across it. Ben reached for Gretchen's hand as they strolled ahead. Calvin walked along next to them. Jesus and Lydia followed along about twenty feet behind. Apologetically Jesus reached for Lydia's hand. Understanding, she allowed him to take it. He smiled and began to swing their joined hands between them as they continued their stroll.

When all returned to the house, people quietly settled into their individual evening routines. Calvin and Gretchen headed toward the showers. Lydia made some check-in phone calls. Jesus sat down with a book in the living room, while Ben turned on the television for the late news. This older TV had no captioning capabilities, and Jesus glanced at Ben, wondering how much of the Spanish broadcast he was understanding.

The first news story was about the rumbling of Irazu earlier in the day. Apparently, the mountain had continued to rumble for several hours, and there was a measurable amount of ash released, but it was not noticeable in Cartago or the capital. The second news story concerned a bill before the legislature. After a series of advertisements, it was the third story which made Ben and Jesus sit up straight in their respective lounge chairs.

It was the images that caught the attention of both. Jesus started to translate the commentary for Ben as the story unfolded. "An unusual incident took place in the early afternoon at *Parque Nacional* where a poor family reported being harassed by school girls and prostitutes as they ate lunch. They called the tourist police number for help and reported to the officers who came that their lunch baskets had been a gift from someone in a passing van. The school-girls had approached the family about half way through their meal, accusing them of stealing the baskets. When the protests increased in volume, local street walkers joined the argument. The police questioned all involved and carefully examined the contents of the baskets. It was when they had emptied the baskets and taken out the cloth lining the bottom that they found an electronic bug. When that was found, the prostitutes and school girls quickly left the scene. The police took the family to *La Guardia* Hospital for observation, but as of this time they have had no negative effects from eating the gift baskets."

By this time, the whole party was glued to the television. A few stray comments about the situation were made, but more thoughts were left unspoken. The last comment was from Jesus. "I'm glad we changed vehicles."

CHAPTER 11

Saturday morning dawned with rain falling on the metal roof. Calvin was the first up and started frying some ham and eggs and warming buttered bread in the oven. Gretchen soon joined him. Lydia began to set the table and Jesus joined her, adding the silverware. Ben was the last one out. He poured juice into glasses, while others put the rest of the food on the table. Breakfast was a cheerful meal with discussion centering on the plan for the day. No one mentioned the newscast of the last night, though Lydia and Jesus had a quiet discussion on the back patio when the meal was over.

The plan for the day was to be tourists. A peaceful morning on the beach, as soon as the rain passed, included looking for shells, tickling toes in the ocean, and renting a leaky paddleboat which got everyone wet. After a stroll on the long pier, they found a small sandwich shop for lunch. Another walk on the beach left everyone tired enough for an afternoon nap.

After their nap, Gretchen, Ben, and Cal asked for permission to take a walk without a bodyguard. Lydia had seen no sign of a tail, so she consented. She knew Ben had his phone just in case. She pulled a plastic chair outside and under the car covering. Sitting there she could watch anyone approaching from the beach or the town, though she didn't expect to see anyone except the Parks returning.

About twenty minutes after she sat down, Jesus came

out, running a comb through his thick black hair. He smiled down at Lydia. "Did you let the kids out by themselves?"

Lydia nodded.

"I think that is safe. I am also thinking about escaping, if I may."

Lydia waited for his explanation.

"The local Catholic church has a Saturday evening service." He pointed to a spire rising just a few blocks away. "Since I do not know what tomorrow may bring, I would like to go to mass tonight. It will probably not be longer than forty-five minutes."

Lydia sighed.

"Would you like to go with me?"

She shook her head. "No, I had better stay here. The Parks should be returning soon." Lydia knew that she wasn't mentioning the main reason she didn't want to go.

"I will miss you, but I understand," said Jesus. He bent and dropped a kiss on the top of Lydia's head. She gave a little start, but quickly remembered her part and smiled broadly up at him. Jesus turned and waved at the little lady who was standing in the doorway across the street. Then he walked up the street.

Lydia continued to sit quietly for a while. Then she noticed that the little lady across the street was still watching her. She smiled and waved, somewhat like Jesus had done. However, the reaction of the lady was not what she had expected. The lady frowned and made what appeared to be a rude gesture. Then she came out, crossed the street and started lecturing Lydia rapidly in Spanish. Lydia, whose Spanish was limited, could not follow what she was saying, though she did make out *hombre*, *mal*, and *iglesia*. She spread her arms, shook her head and apologized for not understanding. The woman repeated much of what she had said before making a dismissive wave and retreating to her home.

By the time Lydia decided that the woman for some reason did not approve of her supposed relationship with Jesus, she also realized that he had been gone for over 45 minutes and the Parks had not returned. She walked to the end of the street and looked up and down the beach. No familiar figures. She walked up the other way until she could see the church. The sidewalk in front of the church was empty. The muscles around her heart tightened. Where was everyone?

Lydia picked up the pace as she walked back toward the house. A quick check of the house confirmed that she had not missed anyone's return. She pulled out her phone and called Ben's number. No answer. She went to the front door. What should she do? How long should she wait before she phoned to report them missing? Why had she let Jesus go off by himself? Why had she let the Parks leave without her? What should she do now?

She knew what the Parks – and Jesus for that matter – would do. They would pray. But why would God listen to her? For their sakes He might listen. "Oh God," she began. Just then she heard the sound of laughter outside her door. Opening it, she saw all four of the missing turn into the drive in front of the house. Her breath escaped in a sigh of relief.

As she smiled her greeting, she wondered if she should tell them about her panic. Not all of it, she decided. "It's good to see you!" she declared. "I was getting a little worried."

Ben glanced at his watch, "We have been gone a while, haven't we."

Jesus looked concerned, "I should have called or had

Ben call."

Yes, you should have, thought Lydia, but she said, "It's OK. Everyone's safe."

"Last time we get out without a guard, I'll bet," commented Calvin. "Especially when I bring up what I thought about during the church service."

Lydia started. "You all were at the Catholic church?" she asked.

"Well," drawled Ben, "we had followed the beach for a ways and then decided to see if we could find a new place to eat supper. We did – a nice fish place – and then continued along the road back this way." Ben was pointing to indicate the directions as he talked.

"As we got close, we saw the church just a little farther down," continued Calvin. "With people going in for evening mass."

"We continued toward the church, when – "Gretchen started.

Jesus finished for her. "When who would they meet along the way, but me!"

"It was nice to have a Catholic with us to give us the meaning of parts of the service," Gretchen affirmed.

"I don't think any of us thought about how long we had been gone or that you thought we were wandering around alone at sunset."

Lydia closed her eyes and sighed.

"Oh, dear," exclaimed Gretchen, "you were worried!"

"Just a little on edge." Lydia set her jaw firmly. "I didn't come all this way to lose you." She forced a smile. "Problem is, now I've got my adrenaline up, trying to decide if I should be contacting anyone. Now *I* need a walk."

Jesus charmingly took her arm. "No problem. Ben will guide us all back to the seafood restaurant."

"Before you do," Calvin broke in, "I don't know if this was an inspiration I had during the service - or if I was day-dreaming because I couldn't understand all of what was said."

"Go ahead," urged his mother.

Cal looked at Jesus and then at Lydia. "How well do you know Jaime?"

"Jaime?" Lydia responded first. "Not at all. I met him at the embassy. He was the driver given to you by the embassy, correct?" She looked at Jesus.

Jesus frowned. "I know some people from the embassy. People I have worked with before. And I have always thought that their security process was sound." He paused, as they all re-thought through the morning when Jaime had appeared at Calvin's front door.

CHAPTER 12

Corvina (sea bass), *pargo* (red snapper), and tuna were shared around the table. Fried *plátanos* joined the rice and beans on their plates. The drinks added color to the table with an assortment of *jugos naturales* in a variety of fruit flavors. As they slowly savored a desert of flan, Ben turned to Jesus. "Do most Catholics in Costa Rica have the attitude you do about Protestants?"

"Oh, *señor*, I do not know percentages. I know that, since many non-Catholic churches are growing, there is sometimes a jealousy by some priests. And, of course, the laws favor Catholicism; it is our official religion."

"Something that is foreign to people from the U.S." said Cal.

"Yes, but a part of our tradition." Jesus emphasized. "My childhood priest was not jealous, however. He had been deeply involved the Ecumenical Peace Movement of the Catholic Church - which began in the 60's at the Second Vatican Council."

"Peace is important to Costa Ricans." This from Lydia.

"Yes. Father Herrera felt deeply that it should be a part of our faith also. He came away with a deepened respect for the non-Catholics he worked with. He told us frequently that the Protestants were reminding us to study and follow the Bible, and told us that they had thanked the Catholics in the group for preserving the Bible through the

Dark Ages."

Ben nodded his agreement. Lydia watched the faces of this group discuss the forbidden subject of religion. She saw no judgmental or argumentative spirits among them.

Jesus continued. "Then he would point to the crucifix and say, 'Every time you see this in the front of our churches, remember that our relationship with God is primary, and that that relationship is possible because of the one who died on the cross.' He would add, 'Every time you see the empty Protestant crosses remember that Jesus not only died, but exhibited power over sin and death by His resurrection. He did not stay dead!'"

"I like that priest!" declared Ben.

"And I am glad we went tonight with you to mass," added Gretchen, "but I do wish that we could go to a service from our own tradition tomorrow."

"In English, Mom?" cautioned Calvin.

The waiter was just passing their table as Gretchen spoke. "I could not help overhearing, *señora*," he said. "There is a Baptist church in town. It is not large, but the pastor has a short English service before the regular service."

"That's my folks – Baptist!" exclaimed Calvin in surprise.

Continuing, the waiter pointed to a bulletin board and said, "I think they have posted their schedule over there."

Jesus popped up and went to look. "*A la diez de la mañana* – ten in the morning."

All eyes looked at Lydia. She shrugged and nodded. "But this time I go with you," she said.

It was while they were walking back to their house that Lydia's call was returned about Jaime. She dropped a little bit behind the others to have a short conversation with whoever was on the other end of the line. When she rejoined the group she looked puzzled.

"What can you tell us, Lydia?" asked Jesus as he dropped into step with her.

"Nothing about Jaime." she said, shaking her head. "He either is legit and undercover in some way, or he's a plant; they are not going to tell us. But…"

"But what?" asked Gretchen, suddenly tense.

"But they raided the resort where we stayed last night … Arrested a couple of those Dons that were there for some 'meeting.' And some call girls. That's all I know. They were glad that we had not been there."

The rest of the evening was spent quietly by the members of the party, each doing whatever he or she needed to do to get ready for the next day. Some washed out clothes, others washed themselves. Gretchen drug out an iron and ironing board from a closet and tried to make her skirts look like they had not been in a suitcase all week. Everyone except Lydia formed a prayer circle before retiring to their rooms, but Lydia sat close enough to listen. In the back of everyone's minds that night were questions about Jaime and the raid on the resort.

Lydia got up at first light; by 7 a.m. all were up and casually dressed. Good Costa Rican bread and a little coffee were enough for now. They decided to walk the beach. It helped; all felt calmer upon their return, so Gretchen whipped up some omelets. Just quiet chatter over the eggs, no one mentioned Jaime or the raid on the resort. No one turned on the television. After breakfast, all examined their limited wardrobes to figure out what to wear to church.

At five till ten, the group hesitantly walked through the open doors of *Iglesia Bautista*. A few people were arranging flowers, distributing song books, and herding children toward rooms in the back; but no one sat in the pews. Leading the way, Calvin walked the small group about a third of the way toward the front of the small sanctuary and eased to the far end of the pew to leave room for the rest of the group. They all filed in and sat down quietly. A couple of the helpers looked up, smiled at the group, and scurried off into the back rooms.

A minute later a smiling young man entered. *"Buenos dias,* hello!" he greeted them. "I apologize that I was not in here when you arrived. Are you here for our English service?"

The row nodded. Ben stood up and spoke. "We are in town for the week and were told that you had an English service at ten?"

"Yes, we do, unfortunately our regular attenders are sick, on vacation, or helping with children's classes, but I would still like to ... *Jesus Caldarón?"*

Jesus had stood up next to Ben, grinning, "Yes, it is. I can't believe that Victor Salas is now a *padre!"*

"Un padre – no! *Hermano,* Jesus, *hermano."*

"So you are a monk?"

Victor laughed and shook his head. "So have you become a Baptist, Jesus?"

"No, but my friends here are, and I understand that Baptists follow the same one that I am named after."

"Claro, Jesus, claro."

Pastor Victor moved up to the front of the church and pulled a chair off the stage. He pushed it up toward the front pew, while motioning them to join him. As they moved Jesus explained the interaction to his companions.

"Victor and I were classmates at the university together."

"We were," Victor affirmed.

"I'm not sure I remember every class we took together, but I know we took four years of English together."

"Which explains why you would have an English service," added Calvin.

"Yes." Victor nodded.

"But what we most remember is a friendly on-going religious debate."

"I'm glad you added friendly, Jesus," said Victor. "It never works to debate beliefs with someone that you don't like."

Jesus turned toward Victor with a look of awe on his face. "I'd never thought about it that way, *Hermano Victor*, but you are right. I knew that I liked and respected you, but there were times that I thought you were just trying to convert me."

"Of course I was, Jesus; but that is because I still have problems believing that Catholics might get to heaven – and I want my friends in heaven with me."

Jesus broke into a big grin. "I am glad that I had the priest I did, because he helped me realize that it is our relationship with – my namesake – that is most important in our journey to heaven. So, even Baptists might get there."

Victor laughed out loud. Then Jesus made introductions.

"Friends," Victor said, "It is obvious that no one else is going to join us, so I think we will make our service less formal. Let's sit together and open our service with a song we all know. Have you had a chance to look at our English songbook?"

Gretchen handed a book to Jesus. "I think we know most of these, so would you see what you know?" Jesus found several that he knew, either from Catholic mass or from listening to Christian music.

After a couple of songs and a little more conversation, Victor asked, "Can I pray for you now?"

Lydia's mouth dropped open in surprise, but everyone else nodded and bowed their heads.

Victor began to pray. "Lord, we are thankful right now for this chance meeting. Though, knowing you, it may not be chance at all. Today I pray for the Parks from the United States. I pray that *Señora* Parks will find her strength renewed and rise up like the powerful eagle. I pray that *Señor* Parks will have the wisdom of Solomon, and that their son Calvin will find your path for him through the jungle of life. For *Señorita* Lydia, the one you have made to be about justice and truth, I pray that you will make her a positive force throughout her life; and for my friend Jesus today I pray for his safety and protection."

Lydia observed Victor closely as the prayer ended. Had she missed something? Jesus had not mentioned anything about their jobs or the reason they were in town in his introduction. And why did he pray for Jesus' safety and not the Parks? She shook her head silently. Why was she worrying about this, since she thought prayer was no more than wishful thinking anyway.

Victor said, "I think I will present the sermon more like it was a Sunday School lesson that we can discuss if it is all right with you."

"Sounds good," replied Ben.

"The scriptures for the morning are Isaiah 61:1 and Luke 4:18. I chose both because our Lord is quoting the Old Testament scripture in the gospel of Luke."

"I'll read it," said Jesus. "The Spirit of the Sovereign LORD is on me, because the LORD has anointed me to preach good news to the poor. He has sent me to bind up the brokenhearted, to proclaim freedom for the captives and release from darkness for the prisoners…"

"It's good to remember that Jesus was interested in the poor, the broken hearted, the captives and the prisoners," Ben said.

"It's good to remember that Jesus also wanted us to be interested in these people," added Gretchen.

"Mom's always helping someone," said Calvin.

"And Jesus thought to give our picnic to those beggars…" Gretchen replied.

"Way to go, Jesus!" This from Victor. "With you all, I don't have to preach – just let you go and you preach to me!" He turned to Lydia, "I have the feeling – I think it is from God – that you have made many sacrifices to help the poor and captives."

"I don't know that I …" Lydia began.

Jesus interrupted. "This passage isn't just about food baskets for the poor," he said. "It said 'to heal the broken hearted.'"

"If anyone …" Lydia stopped and shook her head.

Gretchen and Ben glanced at each other.

Calvin continued. "There is more than one kind of captive. Some are held captive by emotional problems … some are held captive by the prejudices of others … some are held captive by drug habits."

Victor noticed a subtle change in Lydia's bearing.

"May I tell you of some captives in our little community?" asked Victor.

They nodded.

"I will back up a little to make sure you understand … You may know that some years back, Costa Rican school girls started being recruited to … uh … serve some of the less moral tourists." Victor noticed the grim looks before him. "Our government took a variety of actions to stop this

– this unfortunate situation." He sighed. "In recent months
... there has again ... been an increased recruitment ... with
a sad twist. Some of the girls have disappeared completely.
Some ... including two related to families in our church."

"Oh!" Gretchen gasped.

"May we now pray for you, sir?" asked Ben.

The young preacher nodded.

Ben reached out and put his hand on Victor's shoulder. Other's bowed their heads. Lydia hesitated, but joined
them. "Our powerful, righteous heavenly father," began
Ben strongly, "sometimes you are the only one who can
change an evil situation. You changed one for millions of
people when Jesus died for our sins; now, we need you to
change one here. We don't know what exactly has happened to these girls, but it sounds – it sounds like the work
of Evil. Lord, we pray for YOUR power to remove any
power evil has in this situation; and we pray for protection
for those who have been made captive in this. And we pray
this whether it is a captivity of force or a captivity of deception. In Jesus' Name we pray."

"*Amén.*" Jesus and Victor spoke together.

CHAPTER 13

Lydia watched Calvin and Jesus peddling a paddle-boat while Gretchen and Ben strolled on the beach. She lounged in a beach chair under a rented umbrella, but did not feel as relaxed as she looked. Her sunglasses hid her tears. How could Jesus feel so calm? How could Gretchen look so refreshed? Sure, she had taken a two hour nap this afternoon, but Lydia had rested also; and she was almost a basket case.

Yes, she remembered her training about foreign visits: how the energy expenditure is higher and more draining when dealing with foreign languages and foreign customs. For her, not only was she dealing with another country's culture; but also, she was dealing with a bunch of religious fanatics! Why did that church service – if it could be called that – affecting her so strongly? Victor had identified her as a seeker for justice, and that is what she wanted to be so badly! And then there were those poor missing girls.

Why didn't people realize that prostitution was *not* something that women or girls chose from among a wide selection of choices? They were either truly captives, or they felt that they had no other choices. Why did she have the feeling that drugs were involved here, too? Because drugs were so often used to control new "recruits." She knew that.

Why did Jesus need prayers for his safety? Hadn't he already recovered from the attack at the bank? Why did she feel so uncomfortable with him talking about his faith – him more than the Parks? She almost wished sometimes that he would take a little more advantage of the fact that they were supposed to be boyfriend and girlfriend. He was good looking, mannerly, and kind ...

She wiped a couple of tears from under her glasses. The sun was glowing; the water shimmering; the birds flew overhead; and the street vendors were calling out their wares. A shaved ice might be nice.

Lydia flagged down one vendor as he went past and ordered a *granizado con leche*. As the vendor shaved the ice from a large block in his cart, the rest of the group joined her. Each had an order for the vendor which kept him busy for several minutes and significantly diminished his ice block. But it also increased his income for the afternoon.

They found a stone table in the shade of some palms and enjoyed the cool sweetness of the snow cones. The sun was low in the sky, indicating that it would soon be suppertime. Jesus and Calvin elected to walk to a small *soda* between their house and the church which should have a few sandwiches and drinks for their evening meal. Gretchen, Ben, and Lydia returned to the house to clean up from the beach.

Ben turned the television on for the first time that day. He flipped the channels until he found one in English originating from Chicago. After watching the news on that channel for a few minutes, he turned toward Gretchen who was just joining him and said, "All of this news about the States seems so far away. It's hard to remember that it has been less than a week since we were watching this same show in our own living room."

Gretchen smiled, patted his knee, and sat down next to him. The news reporter continued his report. "In other news, Philip Camron was arrested while vacationing in a Costa Rican mountain resort. The report is that some very young women who were in his presence were taken in for questioning. Philip Camron has been expanding the scope of Camron Enterprises, based here in Chicagoland, in recent months. An official statement released by the company says that he was in Costa Rica to negotiate new business contracts with local suppliers."

Gretchen frowned. "Is he vacationing or here on business?"

Ben added, "And why the young girls?"

Gretchen said what all three were thinking, "I sure hope it's not what Victor was talking about in church this morning." She sighed heavily.

"They were arrested," Lydia reminded them. "And the joint drug task force is involved. If there are underage girls ... maybe this will be a break, the beginning of a change for the good."

"An answer to prayer," said Ben.

Unreasonably, Lydia found herself tearing up again. She turned her head away, just as the door opened. Calvin and Jesus' entrance covered a quick wipe away of those tears.

"*Sandwiche de jamón*,'" announced Jesus holding up ham sandwiches.

"*Papas* - chips - and melon!" added Cal.

Gretchen clapped her hands. "Oh that sounds perfect!"

They quickly set out plates and ate their simple supper. Afterwards, Cal and Ben quietly read. Gretchen got ready for an early bedtime. Jesus walked by himself along the beach for a while. Lydia remained on guard. When Jesus returned, he pulled her out the front door and stood with his arm around her shoulder. Turning his head toward hers, he whispered. "Our neighbor has been watching; I thought we needed to keep up appearances." Lydia looked up into his eyes. It might be nice to be his girlfriend, she found herself thinking. She shook herself to clear her head of such thoughts.

"Are you cold, Lydia."

"Not cold, Jesus, just ... just wishing this was simply a vacation, and I could just relax and enjoy the people I am with. They are nice people."

Jesus lifted one eyebrow. "Including me?"

Lydia giggled. "Including you."

"Including all the religious talk?"

Lydia sighed. "Normally I don't like the 'religious talk,' as you put it. However, with the Parks - and with you - it seems genuine, part of who you are." She paused, thinking. "And I'm not anti-religious, just ..."

"Seeking?" Jesus offered.

"Seeking. Hmm. Yes, that fits. Seeking what is actually true, if there is such a thing."

"There is, Lydia, there is." Jesus dropped a kiss on her forehead, waved to the lady peeking through her window across the street, and turned Lydia to go back inside.

CHAPTER 14

When they went inside, the peace of the last few minutes had been shattered. Ben and Calvin were rushing around. Gretchen was nowhere to be seen, but the commotion seemed to be about her. Then a phone rang and Jesus was answering it and talking to someone about the women he had identified earlier. Lydia stopped Ben long enough to ask, "What's wrong with Gretchen?"

"Food poisoning, we think," Ben replied.

"What?"

"She had come out ready for bed, then suddenly turned and rushed toward the bathroom." Ben shook his head. "She didn't quite make it. I've been cleaning up."

"And I've been getting her something to rinse her mouth out with," declared Cal as he went past.

"Not pleasant." Ben grimaced. "Both ends."

"But how is she now?" asked Lydia.

"Too soon to tell. Gretchen has a touchy stomach. Foreign travel usually gets her sooner or later."

"But what could it have been? We all ate the same thing for supper."

"Maybe her piece of ham was cut a little too close to the bone. Maybe it wasn't supper. Don't know. Just trying to take care of her now."

Cal came back into the room. He looked at Jesus. "Can you help me find a place that sells bottled soda and maybe some crackers? I know it is Sunday night, but I think Mom is going to need something..."

"Certainly, Calvin," said Jesus, picking up his light

jacket. "Let us go."

Gretchen came back out to the living room, looking pale but clean. Lydia made a spot for her on the couch, with some pillows. Ben got her i-pod for her to use to read or play games. Expressing her thanks, Gretchen settled down comfortably for about ten minutes. Then, suddenly she popped up and started to the bathroom again. By the time she came out this time, Calvin and Jesus were back with several bottles of ginger ale and a pack of soda crackers.

"The little shop we went to earlier got us these things," said Calvin.

"Yes." Jesus looked a little grim. "They also threw out the rest of the ham which our sandwiches had been made from. They said that they did not want to risk anyone else getting sick. I left a generous tip for opening up for us."

"How are you doing, Mom?" asked Cal.

Gretchen smiled wanly. "Not as well as I'd like. But, the house's plumbing is working very well. For that I am thankful."

She settled again on the couch, with a large cooking pot added to her arsenal, just in case she couldn't reach the bathroom in time. Jesus poured some ginger ale for Gretchen, while Lydia again arranged pillows for her. Ben turned on the television and, after some channel flipping, found an old movie in English that they had seen before.

"Ben knows that when I'm feeling bad, I don't want to be too excited by anything I watch," explained Gretchen.

After a couple more trips to the bathroom, Gretchen seemed more comfortable, sometimes dozing on the couch. The rest met in the kitchen and decided that Lydia would take the first shift and Ben the second, if someone was needed to sit up with Gretchen during the night. Jesus and Cal would be in charge of getting help if an emergency arose.

Jesus also mentioned that he would have to find a way into the capital in the morning to take care of some more business about the women he had identified. He told them that two more who might have been at the bank were being detained. The standing conference ended with a prayer by Ben for his wife and the needs of their little household.

As the rest made their way to bed, Lydia got comfortable in a chair close to Gretchen. Gretchen was dozing again, so Lydia felt able to do the same. The room was lit by a light from the kitchen and the light from the television, which continued to tell its stories quietly throughout the night.

Gretchen felt better in the morning, though still a little weak. Ben poured her some more ginger ale. Lydia, a little stiff from her night sleeping in a chair, stretched and asked Gretchen if there was anything she felt like eating for breakfast. Gretchen smiled quietly and said, "No leftovers."

"Ha!" That was Calvin as he came out of his room. "The few we had went out with the trash this morning."

"What about some good Costa Rican bread, *señora*?" asked Jesus.

"That does sound good," replied Gretchen.

"Sounds good to me also," added Ben.

"I think I have time to accompany Calvin to the little bakery we found the other day," Jesus continued.

"Before?" Gretchen had missed out on the kitchen conversation of the night before.

"Before Jesus returns to San José concerning the women in the bank," Lydia answered.

Gretchen nodded.

Calvin and Jesus took off immediately. Gretchen insisted that she felt well enough to shower and get dressed. While the rest were busy, Ben and Lydia put their heads together to figure out the best plan for the day. Probably a quiet day on the beach, with food cooked at home and plenty of bottled water, just to make sure Gretchen recovered well.

"How long are we going to stay here?" Ben asked.

Lydia looked thoughtful. "I'm not sure. Hopefully,

today will bring some more watersheds in the case and we'll get an all-clear soon. We do have the place rented for a week, and this is not a bad place for a home base while you do some more sightseeing."

Ben cleared his throat. "This has been a much more expensive vacation than we had planned," he said. "However, I feel a little guilty depending completely on Uncle Sam's pockets, especially since those pockets have so many holes in them ... Would it be all right with the powers that be if our next outing came out of our vacation fund?"

Lydia grinned. "I'm sure it would. Uncle Sam would probably appreciate it, if he finds out about it."

Just then Calvin and Jesus came bursting through the door with *Hermano* Victor. Jesus said, "I've found a ride to San José. I won't need to take your SUV."

Calvin continued, "Victor is going to San José with one of his church families to pick up their daughter. One of the missing girls has been found!"

"Praise the Lord!" said Ben.

Tears filled Gretchen's eyes, and Lydia felt the tears well up in hers also.

Victor spoke. "I can take Jesus and bring him home. I would appreciate another driver; the parents will probably not be emotionally prepared to drive today."

Jesus continued, "I was struggling with the idea of leaving you without a car. This solves that problem. If you want to take any trips today, you will be able to."

"I'm going to stay, also, folks," said Calvin. "Jesus won't need me, and they don't want me to go back to my apartment yet."

"Victor will be back with the parents of the recovered girl soon, so I'll have a little breakfast with you all and get ready to go," continued Jesus.

While they were talking Gretchen quietly started boiling water, and Ben set plates on the table. Butter and jelly went on next. A pitcher of milk and glasses were put with them. Cal put tea bags and ground coffee and cloth filters on the table next to cups.

Victor waved good-by. Gretchen brought the boiled water to the table and they ate, after a simple prayer from Ben. Victor returned quickly with an eight-passenger van, and Jesus left with Victor and a couple who sat quietly in the second set of seats.

Victor and Jesus talked in Spanish as Victor drove. After catching up a little more on the ten years that had passed since the two graduated from the university, Jesus turned to the parents. "I am glad that your daughter was found. I cannot imagine how hard the last few days have been for you."

"*Gracias, señor.*" The father spoke in Spanish, too. "We were so afraid that she might never be able to come home again."

The mother sobbed. "We cannot understand what has happened, but we are glad that she was found."

Jesus looked stern. "I am glad too. May the other young lady be found also."

"Yes," said the mother glancing sideways at her husband. "I think it may be harder to bring her home. I believe she thought this was going to be a great adventure ... I don't know when she will realize what danger she is in."

Jesus turned toward Victor. His friend was nodding ever so slightly. Jesus sighed.

After about an hour on the road, Victor pulled off by a small restaurant. All got out to stretch and get a Coke. When they returned to the vehicle, Jesus took over the driving. Victor had been making his winding way up the mountains; now Jesus followed the winding road down. When they reached the city, Jesus skillfully maneuvered through the dense traffic toward the government building that was the destination of all in the car. Jesus parted company with the rest to try to identify the other two who had been picked up, and to give his testimony in the initial hearing of the two women he had identified earlier.

Acting on a last-minute thought, he asked for copies of the mug shots of all four women who had been arrested, including the one he had not been able to identify. Victor and the reunited family were waiting when he got back to the van. Jesus tried not to stare, but noted the tearstained young face which had been scrubbed clean of any sign of makeup. As they drove back through the city, he could hear the quiet conversation the girl was having with her parents.

"I knew that you and Dad were worried about money ... The lady said we would earn as much as a bank president – that we could help our families." There was a hiccupping sound from the backseat. "I thought we could choose whether we, whether we wanted a particular person ... I didn't realize ... "This time she paused quietly for several seconds. "They dressed us up in beautiful gowns with pretty makeup. Then they drugged us. Then they took us to a secluded resort, and there were rich-looking old men there. Then the police came." Quiet sobbing came from the back seat. "Even drugged I was so scared!"

Jesus glanced in the mirror. The parents were comforting their daughter. He noted that a silver Saab had moved into position behind them. Hadn't there been a similar car behind them in downtown San José? About ten minutes later, the Saab passed them and a white Hyundai moved up. Jesus turned his attention back to the conversation, without neglecting the turns and twists in the road.

"Miranda got sick from the drugs. She couldn't wake up. They didn't take her to the party because she couldn't open her eyes. Now I wish they had taken her, because she would be going home too; because the police came."

Jesus and Victor exchanged a sad look. Jesus found himself wondering if the other girl had survived that drug overdose. Then he noticed the white Hyundai was still behind them. He decided to test a question in his mind. An intersection was coming up; he turned on his signal and then turned the van. The Hyundai turned also.

Jesus speed dialed a number on the phone as he drove through a small community. Into the phone he spoke the name of the town and the words "white Hyundai" and then hung up. He pulled into a parking spot in front of a *farmacia*, and asked Victor to go in and buy some wrapped snacks. The Hyundai parked about a block behind them.

While Victor was gone, he asked the girl if she knew the name of the secluded resort where she had been taken. It was the same place he had been with the Parks just a few days ago. When he asked for the location within the resort, it sounded like the very villa where they had stayed. This brought up questions about Jaime again, but he put them aside. There was one more thing he wanted to ask this girl. He reached into his pocket for the photos he had been given, handed them to the back seat, and asked, "Do any of these women look familiar to you?"

The girl looked at the first one and shook her head. That was her response to the second photograph also. On the third picture she paused, frowned, and then shrugged and moved to the last of the four pictures. This fourth photo produced a totally different response. "Felicita!" She turned toward her parents. "Do you remember me telling you about the traveling *soda* that used to stop by our school? This is the lady who ran it." She glanced down at the picture. "What I didn't tell you was that, after a while I found out that she was 'finding' pills for those who wanted them …" Her voice trailed off.

A few tears dropped before the girl could continue. "She is the one … She is the one who started talking about a way to earn a lot of money fast … Then her *brother*…" (This was said sarcastically.) "Her brother came and started trying to 'hire' some of us girls."

"Why didn't you say anything?" asked her mother tearfully.

"Because I thought it was none of my business, at

first," the girl replied. "Later ... it was because I was interested myself – to help our family."

Victor returned to the car just then, bearing bottled water and several packaged snacks.

"I would rather us all starve than for you to sell yourself," declared the father angrily.

Victor, who seemed to understand that part of the conversation immediately, spoke in a soothing tone. "Neither is necessary. Our church community helps those in need, and we are all in need at some time. Maybe now we need to help you. Maybe later you will be the ones helping someone else."

Victor took over the lead of the conversation, while passing out what he had brought, soothing the family and offering words of redemption and hope. As this was happening, Jesus got out his cell phone again and made a call to the police back in San José. "I was not able to identify the fourth woman, and I know that you could not hold her, but it turns out the young girl you released this morning identified her instantly as the one who had sought out young girls..." He listened for a while, responded to questions with a yes or no as they came, and then hung up. By this time the other conversation had ended and all were looking at Jesus. His reply was to the point. "The police know who this woman is now and will be looking for her." Then he drove back to the highway.

Everybody understood that Jesus had asked for help in those phone calls. Victor tried to reassure the family, but Jesus knew that he was also puzzled by the events. Jesus tried to explain, without saying too much. "I believe that there is a white car behind us – now behind us about three cars – that is following us. There was another car that followed us all through San José. What I don't know is whether the car follows us because of your situation or because of the testimony I gave in court today." He wondered if the two were related, but didn't speak his thoughts on that point. "I hope soon some law enforcers will join us and stop the car."

The three in the back seat turned to watch the traffic behind them. Victor leaned toward Jesus and murmured, "And these law enforcers you have on speed dial on your phone."

Jesus glanced at him. "I never thanked you for your prayer for my safety yesterday, Victor. I do thank you."

Over the next ten minutes, the white Hyundai slowly crept closer to their van again. When it was once again right behind them, Jesus got a call on his phone. Victor held the phone to his ear so he could keep both hands on the wheel. "A red convertible ... yes." Victor noticed the convertible in the left lane in front of them. "Blue truck ..." Victor saw a beat-up old truck right behind the Hyundai. "Black limo ..." The black limousine sat just ahead of them. "*Claro. Gracias.*"

The white Hyundai turned on its signal and moved to the left lane. The truck slowly started to edge over also. The Hyundai accelerated until it was even with their van. Jesus noted a metallic glinting movement from the passenger's side. Victor called out, "*En el nombre de Jesus!*" just as Jesus stepped on the brakes. The van decelerated quickly. The limo slid into the spot vacated by the van. The other side was sealed by the side of a mountain.

The three law enforcement vehicles slowly put a squeeze play on the white car, until all were stopped on the side of the mountain. Officers jumped out; machine guns appeared; then handcuffs were snapped around the wrists of three men from the white car before they were even standing outside the vehicle.

Victor swung his head around to look behind them. Where was the rest of the traffic?

Jesus answered his unspoken thought. "Police road-block down below. They are telling people there has been an accident." Sobbing sounded from the back seat. Jesus glanced back and tried to reassure them. "The bad guys are caught. We are going to be all right."

Two officers strolled back toward the car. Jesus got out and talked in quiet tones with them, then one officer returned with him to the van. The officer explained what was going to happen. "We are taking the suspects back to the capital. A little way ahead there is a restaurant. You will stop there for lunch. By the time you finish, there will be a taxi ready to take you home."

"A taxi? But that is so expensive!" declared the father.

"Do not worry, *señor*; it is paid for."

"But are we safe?" asked the mother.

The police officer paused before he spoke. "We believe so ... This may sound strange, but we do not think you were the targets."

"Mistaken identity?" asked the girl.

Another pause. "Perhaps. We will be investigating to be sure." Victor was staring hard at Jesus, while the officer continued, "*Señor* Caldarón will drive back with Roberto up there in the pickup truck. There will not be room for him in the taxi."

Victor spoke quietly under his breath to Jesus. "*Vaya con Dios, mi amigo.*"

"*Gracias, Hermano* Victor," said Jesus with a thoughtful smile.

They had arrived at the restaurant by this time. It was owned by a family from the Caribbean side of Costa Rica; their ancestors had been brought to Costa Rica as slaves from Jamaica; and, though they spoke Spanish fluently with their customers, they spoke English to each other. No one felt very hungry with stomachs still in knots, but the thought of Caribbean-style Rice and Beans *con pollo* tempted them in spite of their recent excitement. The spicier version of the Costa Rican staple, with flavorful chicken added, came quickly. They were just finishing as a taxi pulled up.

Again, Victor sent up a quick prayer for his friend, before Jesus headed with one of the police officers to the old pickup. Victor got into the taxi's front seat after helping the family into the back. He put one index finger sideways against his lips and nodded to the three frightened people, then nodded at the officers. The second officer who had joined them for lunch got back into the convertible and trailed along behind the small caravan headed toward Puntarenas.

CHAPTER 15

Lydia, Calvin, Ben, and Gretchen spent a quiet morning at their rented house. However, by 11:00 a.m. Gretchen declared that she was feeling claustrophobic and would at least like a car ride. This was about the time that Jesus had been testifying against the women in San José.

Calvin was their driver for the day with Gretchen starting out in the seat next to him. They drove to the point of the peninsula that the town was built on and around on the other side. When they reached the highway out of town, Lydia suggested that they turn around and drive back, this time looking for a place to eat. Though Gretchen was still not feeling up to eating anything adventurous, they found a little place with a luncheon buffet. Gretchen confined herself to rice *sin frejoles* and a small sweet banana while the others ate everything that looked well cooked.

As they sat eating in the open-sided building, Gretchen, still nibbling at her plain rice, noticed a little commercial dock across the street. "Does that sign say 'thirty minute boat rides to San Lucas'?" she asked.

Calvin turned his head and affirmed her translation.

"Why don't we take one?" responded Gretchen.

Ben was concerned. "Are you sure you feel good enough?"

"We have bottled water – and I brought tissues, just in case," replied Gretchen.

"It says that there are boats at least every hour to and from the island." This from Calvin again.

Lydia, who had no desire to return to the house for

the whole afternoon, said, "Well, let's investigate."

The investigation ended with the four boarding a small boat within 15 minutes of Gretchen's original comment. Ben, according to his earlier conversation with Lydia, paid for the trip. The sun was bright; the breeze, delightful. Lydia looked at the bloom in Gretchen's cheeks and was glad they had come. At one point Cal spotted a sea turtle to the left of the boat. Occasionally fish were visible under the water. It didn't seem anytime at all before they arrived at San Lucas. Ben helped his wife off the boat, and she turned to read a sign as Lydia scrambled out.

"Oh my!" Gretchen exclaimed. She turned toward Ben. "We have come to Costa Rica's Alcatraz."

"Sure, Mom, didn't you read the sign at the boat dock?" Calvin asked.

"Oh, I just wanted to take a boat ride. I figured any place in Costa Rica would be beautiful."

Lydia stepped closer. "We can turn around and go right back, Gretchen."

Gretchen shook her head. "No, I'm interested in the history of this country. I've just got to rearrange my thinking about this trip." She reached up and pretended to screw her head on tighter. "There. I'm ready to go."

An hour later found the little group standing in the little chapel that had been a part of the worst prison in the history of Costa Rica. Gretchen sighed. "I know some of these men did terrible things ... but others just seemed to be in the wrong place at the wrong time..."

"-- or made some powerful enemies," added Calvin.

Lydia looked up toward heaven. "Hell in paradise."

"Wherever there are people, there is the potential for that," said Ben.

"Just think how different that short boat ride would be, if you were coming here to die." This from Cal.

Gretchen knelt on the chapel floor. "Lord, there is so much pain in this world. Some we cause ourselves, but much of it is out of our control. You are the healer; you are the redeemer; you are the one who sent Jesus to save us. Help those who are imprisoned: those behind iron bars, in dungeons, and those whose prisons cannot be seen."

Ben cleared his throat and said, "Amen."

Both looked up to see tears streaming down Lydia's cheeks.

The trip back to Puntarenas started out more subdued. Then Calvin noticed a pretty young woman and became quite animated, while Ben peacefully went to sleep. While Calvin conducted a respectful flirtation and Ben snored lightly, Gretchen turned to Lydia. "Thank you for consenting to this trip. It wasn't exactly what I expected, but I'm glad we came."

Lydia was quiet for a moment. "I know that you noticed my tears, Gretchen."

Gretchen nodded, but said nothing.

"I am very sensitive to – I became an agent because –" Lydia sighed. "I grew up in a very middleclass family with great parents." She looked out over the water as she continued. "The thing was, I was adopted into that family when I was three. I have no memories of my life before that, but I think it was pretty ugly."

She looked back at Gretchen. "When I entered the Agency, I looked up my birth family … My mother was a rather pathetic person. Helpless … hopeless. I felt sorry for her.

"It was one of her brothers that gave me the creeps. I have no proof that he ever did anything to me, though doctors have told me – that someone did. I contacted local authorities about my suspicions, and they started watching him." She sucked in air and clenched her teeth. "Now he is serving time for assaulting someone else."

Gretchen laid a hand on Lydia's arm. "I'm glad you were able to stop him."

"Twenty years later." Lydia did not look glad.

"But you did what you could when you could." Gretchen thought for a moment. "You helped God remove a little bit of evil from the helpless."

Lydia examined her hands. "A little bit of evil ... removed ... I hope so."

They were quiet for a while. When Gretchen spoke again, she appeared to be changing the subject. "Ben and I went through a rough time a while back. I went through a rough time. Ben was afraid that if I went for counseling locally, that it would cause gossip in the church. So, I drove an hour to a university town to find a counselor. It was difficult, but it was important. I'm glad I did it."

Lydia continued examining her hands. "Don't worry about me. The CIA keeps a check on its agents. Sessions after every mission. I'll be O.K."

Gretchen watched a seagull fly past. "Though we kept it pretty quiet, I did have a few friends praying for me during that time. I'll be praying for you."

Lydia sounded almost bitter when she spoke again. "Do you consider me a friend? Or do you just say you'll pray for everyone."

Gretchen chose her words carefully. "I probably should be praying for everyone ... I know that you are working – guarding us – but I have come to consider you a friend."

Lydia's voice softened. "Thank you."

They were back on the mainland by three o'clock. By the time Jesus was dropped off, they had returned to the house and were sitting around resting up from their adventure.

CHAPTER 16

"Hola, mis amigos," Jesus called as he entered the front door.

Calvin looked out the window in time to see the beat up old pickup drive off. "What happened to your ride?"

"That is a long story," Jesus replied. "I will tell some of it after I find out how your mother is doing." He turned to Gretchen. "Has a day of rest revived you?"

Gretchen smiled, but it was Ben who answered. "My wife has done a little more than rest today."

Cal cut in. "Yup. Mom's been in prison."

"Prison?" Jesus looked at the smiles all around and suddenly understood. "San Lucas?"

Gretchen nodded. "Yes, I wanted to go for a boat ride."

Jesus' expression became serious. "In that place many died. You have a saying – cruel and unusual punishment. For many San Lucas was that."

He glanced at Lydia and was surprised by her almost savage expression. She saw his surprise. "Cruel and unusual – what is it called when the innocent are given such treatment?"

"Well, *señorita*, I am sure that some of the convicts were innocent, but I do not understand..."

Gretchen broke in. "I think Lydia is thinking about abused children, not the residents of San Lucas Prison."

"Ah," said Jesus, "like the young lady we brought home today."

Lydia's head jerked toward him. "She is safe?"

Jesus inclined his head. "Yes, Lydia, I believe she is safe."

Calvin interrupted. "You said you'd tell us why you left in a van and returned in an old pickup."

"Old pickup?" The response came in unison from the other three in the room.

Jesus gave them a quick outline of the events of the day.

"So who were the bad guys after?" asked Ben.

Jesus shrugged. "I am not sure ... I think it is more likely to be me, but I have found a connection between the two situations."

Lydia sat up. "Are the drug dealers into prostitution also?"

Jesus frowned. "I am not sure about any others, but the fourth lady in the bank appears to be involved with both. Our prodigal daughter identified her from a photo."

"But could she really be sure of a woman she met under such unusual circumstances?"

"That is not where she met the woman. She met her – repeatedly – at a rolling snack shop outside of her school."

An explosive sound escaped from Ben's lips.

Lydia was rigid. "They were recruiting –"

"And supplying," added Jesus.

" – recruiting and supplying drugs to children right outside their school?"

"Sí. Apparently they slowly built relationships with the students, so, by the time they revealed their true purpose, the kids didn't want to betray them."

Gretchen slumped in her chair. She started several times to say something and stopped each time. Finally she said, "God, help remove this evil from the innocent."

They decided to call Pizza Hut for delivery for supper. About an hour after the phone call, a motorcycle with a box on the back drove up and stopped outside their house.

Gretchen poured drinks while Ben doled out the required number of *colones*, including a generous tip for the deliveryman. The pizza was good and not quite as greasy as those in the States. Calvin and Ben had walked down to a small *Super Mercado*, coming back with bananas and cantaloupe.

"An American meal?" asked Jesus.

"Almost," replied Gretchen. "The bananas are sweeter than the large ones we get in the U.S."

As they topped off the meal with coffee beans covered in chocolate, Ben asked, "What next?"

Jesus tipped his chair back and looked at the ceiling. "There were many phone calls and consultations on the way back today, especially after the – police intervention. It was decided that a couple of investigators will come to Puntarenas: one to watch the reunited family and the school and one to watch this house and the community at large. We think that the bad guys will move on, now that their activities have been revealed. But we do not know whether they realize we know what we know, and we do not want to leave this community at the mercy of such people as those who would corrupt their children."

"Good idea," murmured Ben.

"What about us?" asked Cal.

"Tomorrow you will visit another famous volcano in Costa Rica. You will pack your swimsuits and a change of clothes. Everything else, pack up in case someone needs to bring it to you. There are those who are trying to make arrangements at this moment."

"Wow!" Gretchen had not yet gotten used to the process being used to protect them.

Jesus turned to Lydia. "One more day I will be your 'boyfriend,' Lydia, and then our roles will change. I am to be a substitute English teacher in a school in a *barrio* of Tres Rios, between the capital and the city of Cartago. After searching police records and some interviews today, it was discovered that there has been an increase in drug use in this area; and a girl has disappeared from that school also. Maybe my *friend* from the bank will show herself again."

"But if you see her, won't she recognize you?" asked Calvin.

Jesus set his lips in a firm line. "Maybe, but I will ask *Hermano* Victor to pray for my safety again."

"And we will too," declared Gretchen.

CHAPTER 17

The next morning they all headed North and then East until they saw the almost perfect cone of the Arenal Volcano rising southeast of them. The top of the peak was shrouded in a flat, wispy cloud which they realized was actually not water vapor but volcanic smoke. Soon they came to a forested area. They drove through that for a short distance until they came to a parking lot. Jesus went to check on the bus schedule back to San José, while Ben and Lydia argued over who would pay for the day at the spa.

Tall trees stretched overhead; bubbling brooks ran through a park of exotic flowers. The main brook was actually a hot spring with steam rising over lush foliage. People swam in natural-looking pools along the course of the brook with Arenal rising above it all. Gretchen didn't wait long to get out her camera and start taking photographs. They walked the paths, lounged along the stream watching monkeys scampering overhead, and then changed into bathing suits for a steamy dip.

Lydia felt herself relaxing as she sat on a rocky ledge under a waterfall shower. She looked around at her friends and realized it would be easy to forget why she was there. She forced herself to scan the area and note the behavior of each guest. She was dividing her attention between this and just enjoying the warm water when she noticed a movement on her right. Her attention followed the movement, but she relaxed as she recognized Jesus joining her under the waterfall. Smiling, she continued to look around.

"I will be going soon, Lydia," Jesus said.

Lydia felt unexplainably sad.

"A bus to San José leaves in an hour. Except for a few dead spots on the way, you should be able to reach me by phone."

Lydia nodded.

"In the morning, I start teaching English at a school in the San Diego *Barrio*." He kicked his feet. "I won't take calls during school, but you can text. I'll answer when I can."

Lydia wondered why he was telling her all this, but she knew Jesus had become an integral part of the adventure. "You will be missed." That was all she could think to say.

Knowing that it would be a late night, Jesus slept during the bus ride back to San José. He picked up clothes and a few other necessities from his apartment, got keys and memory cards for his phone/camera from another agent, and took a late bus toward Tres Rios. Finally, the bus stopped near the entrance to a gated community, but the gate hung open. Jesus walked through the gate and along the street which led up the hill toward a school. When he reached the end of the street, he turned to his left. There on the corner was a dark house with a *SE VENDE* sign in the front window.

Jesus fit a key into the lock of the barred fence. The gate swung open with a grating sound. Jesus locked the gate behind him. Another key opened the house's front door. He flipped on a light. Sheets hung over the windows for curtains. Folding chairs and a small television set passed as living room furniture.

Jesus passed through the other rooms. The kitchen held a small refrigerator which had been stocked with a few necessities and a microwave. The bathroom contained the required toilet paper and trash can and towels. Another room contained a backpack filled with school supplies. Up the stairs he found two other small bedrooms. One was completely empty except for a picture of the Virgin on one wall. The other had a blow-up mattress on the floor, sheets, blankets, and a pillow. "The necessities, nothing more." Jesus spoke to empty walls. He hoped that he would not have to stay here long. He adjusted the sheet hung over the window, made his humble bed, and soon lay down upon it.

Jesus had been used to living alone, but after the past week he found himself feeling lonely that night. He got up and took the sheet down from the window, so he could see the stars. "*Señor*, I will need your help for this," he said in prayer. "Also, please, guide and protect the people I am missing tonight." He turned over and was soon asleep.

Sunlight shown through the uncovered window, waking Jesus up before 6 a.m. He took his clothes downstairs, quickly showered, and ate something cold in the refrigerator for breakfast. Picking up an umbrella to ward off the light drizzle that was falling, he strode up the hill to the small high school set in a clearing on the mountainside.

Turning around, he gazed at the community below him. Over to the right, across the highway, he could see Terra Mall. In front of him, he could see the large, dark factory building which provided low-paying jobs to many in the surrounding area. Across the street, small shop keepers were opening their specialty shops, most of them selling one kind of food. To the left, he saw the one-story tiny dwellings of those who had left the crowded squalor of San José's poorer districts only to bring much of it along with them. In spite of that, it was a place of hope. People moved purposefully along the streets, sidestepping puddles and pooches to reach the bus stops.

A motorcycle wove its way out of this region, past the corner store by the entrance to the gated community, and up the hill toward the school. Jesus saw the driver wave at several students as he got closer. The motorcycle stopped across from the house that Jesus was staying in and opened a container set over the back wheel, like the pizza delivery man had used. Jesus couldn't see what was in the box, but students dressed in their school uniforms were stopping by the motorcycle, giving the driver some money, and walking away drinking and eating something. It looked like coffee and bread of some kind.

Jesus turned to enter the school. Actually, since the walkways were only covered, not enclosed, he was just walking along a path toward a door marked *OFICINA*. After a bit, he found someone who understood why he was there and led him to his classroom. It was obvious that substitute teachers were a rarity; usually students were left to shift for themselves if the regular teacher got sick.

Of course Jesus knew that the regular English teacher wasn't sick, but had been given a paid vacation so that Jesus would have a "cover" for his surveillance. He looked over the notes left by the teacher, wrote assignments on the board, along with his name, and turned to find his students entering the room.

The students stopped their chatter as they entered the room. "*¿Donde esta la Señora Zamora?*" one asked.

Jesus replied, "In English, please."

"*¿Por qué?*" another student responded.

"Because this is a fourth year English class, and, if you cannot talk in English by now, you have not been listening to your teacher."

He heard someone mumbling, but he ignored it.

"To answer your question, I do not know where your teacher is. All I know is that I was asked to substitute for her until she returns."

Eyes opened wide. Jesus knew that they were not used to substitute teachers, but he determined to keep them on task, if possible. "*Siéntense por favor.*"

Students made their way to their seats. Jesus returned to speaking English. "Today we will pretend that we are working as tour guides for English-speaking tourists."

"Cool," someone said.

"The purpose of this lesson is to help us to realize that

speaking English well can open up many job opportunities for you. Besides tourism, jobs in our Peace Initiatives require English competency." He paused and decided to take a bold step. "Even those of you who may wish to take up a life of crime – speaking English opens up opportunities to work with U.S. criminal organizations."

Laughter rippled through the room.

The next period Jesus met a younger second year class. He switched to speaking Spanish. Most of this class was very modest and respectful, though he noticed two girls and one young man who seemed to be trying to act more grown up than they actually were. The girls' uniform skirts had been rolled up at the waist so that they would be shorter. The young man slouched and pulled his pants low on his hips. Jesus did not comment on these things, but made mental notes.

The day continued through more classes of various levels. Finally, the last class left and the teachers could leave for lunch. Jesus knew that he was supposed to journey further up the hill to the elementary school, so he looked around for a way to get a quick bite before his afternoon started. He noticed the motorcycle was back across the road from his house.

Trotting down the hill, he stood in line behind a couple of students. The cyclist was chatting comfortably with the students, but the students seemed uncomfortable with Jesus' presence. The students got sandwiches and soft drinks and left. The cyclist said, "*Jamón o pollo?*"

"*Jamón, por favor, y ...*" Jesus looked in the box. "Sprite."

"*Muy bien, señor.*"

Jesus paid the price mentioned and moved toward the path up to the school. He was mentally reviewing what he had seen in the box. There had been a couple more wrapped sandwiches and cans of pop. There had been a few small items, maybe candy bars or something similar. It was not what he had seen that had raised a red flag. Even if he had not known about the situation in Puntarenas, he would have wondered at the uncomfortable postures of the students as he walked up. He made a mental note to ask the other teachers about the motorcycle food business.

That evening, Jesus walked to the corner *pulperia*. The Chinese owner scurried around inside keeping an eye on the customers. Jesus picked out a few items, ending with a popsicle from the freezer on one side of the store. As he turned, he saw the proprietor hurrying past him. In fluent Spanish she was scolding someone behind him. He turned and saw the three students he had noted for their deviant dress earlier in the day.

"You are not shopping, so leave!" said the Chinese lady. "We are a legitimate business, not a place for people like you!"

The young people looked belligerent, but Jesus was most disturbed by the bold glance one teenage girl gave him as she was shooed out of the store. He paid for his items and started back toward his lodging. Across the street from the store, he saw the youths talking to someone on a motorcycle. Was it the vendor from whom he had bought his lunch? The person had a helmet on, so Jesus couldn't tell. The popsicle didn't taste quite as sweet as he had expected as he ate it on the way back to the house.

Before turning in for bed, he made a few calls. His superiors would want a report, though most of what he had to report was just an uncomfortable feeling. Only one suspect had shown himself, but there were three children who appeared to be in danger. Would he be told to wait or act quickly? And what could he do on just suspicions?

CHAPTER 18

In the morning there was a text from Lydia. "Return-ing to Central Valley tomorrow. Parks would like 2 c u @ mall. Is that possible? Time?"

Jesus replied, "Will check. Back 2 u later."

He finished getting ready for school and walked up the hill again. That morning his assignment for the students was to get in groups of two or three and develop a dialog about an employment situation where they might need Eng-lish. It was in his second hour class that things got interest-ing. One group acted out a scene in a tourist shop. Another demonstrated working in the airport. It was the third group that had Jesus furtively turning on the camera in his smart phone to record the presentation.

The baggy pants boy got up and, in fairly under-standable English, said, "Hello, I am a tourist from North America. I am very rich."

Then the short-skirted girl walked up wiggling her hips. "Hello, Mister," she said.

"Wow, you are beautiful!" said Mr. Tourist. "How much money to have your body for one hour?"

Giggles and snorts filled the room. Jesus thought about calling a halt to this, but decided to handle it a differ-ent way. He was silent for the moment.

The girl batted her eyes and cocked her head to one side. "You think I am cheap, mister?"

"No, I do not think you are cheap, but I must have you!" The boy continued. "How about $5,000 U.S. dollars?"

The girl smiled and hooked her arm in his while saying, "That is very generous."

Laughter and clapping ensued as the two made their way back to their seats.

Jesus clicked the off button on his smart phone and slid it back into his pocket. "Fairly good English pronunciation," he stated in a flat tone. "The phrasing was a little awkward, but understandable." He looked straight at the girl. "I do need to correct a bit of your situation however. A prostitute on her own would never get a price like that for an hour, and if she had a pimp or a madam to promote her, she would have to share with them. In fact, that kind of price is a very rare situation for a whore. When it is charged, it is usually someone else getting most of it."

He turned to look at the boy. "Men who buy women by the hour are, in my opinion, scum. They are not remembering that every woman is someone's daughter, or sister, or mother. Would we laugh if it was our mother who had to make her living that way? Or our daughter?" He shook his head. "I hope none of you ever have to know English for the situation we just saw. It would be a very sad day."

Most of the room looked somber by now, though the two were still smirking. Jesus noticed later as the class left the room that the second young woman who had rolled her skirt to make it look shorter had unrolled it. She glanced at him briefly as she passed out the door with a scared look in her eyes. Before the next class, Jesus took out his phone and sent the video to his superiors, along with a note about the situation.

The rest of the morning went fairly well. He'd thought about packing a lunch, but decided to risk the motorcycle entrepreneur again. Again, it seemed to Jesus that the students stopped their conversations when he stepped close. Of course students were often uncomfortable around teachers after school. That could be all it was.

His choices were ham and beef today. He ordered the beef and asked if he could have some of the little candies or cakes to go with it. The seller shook his head. "Sorry," I have no more cakes today," he said. "Ask again tomorrow."

Jesus paid, thanked the man, and turned toward his home-of-the-moment. Inside he ate the sandwich with a glass of milk from his refrigerator. He carefully saved the wrapper of the sandwich. Before he headed back up to the school, he took a small kit from the back of the fridge and wiped the outside of the sandwich wrapper. In one area, there was a color change to the paper. He took a photo, sent photo and text to his supervisor, and headed back up for his afternoon at the elementary school. He was late, but under the circumstances, he felt he had made the right decision to take the time he had.

***

Strange, Gretchen almost felt like she was coming home as she reentered the Central Valley of Costa Rica. She recognized various parks and buildings as they made their way into and through the capital. They stopped at a three story mall not too far from Calvin's apartment for lunch and a walk, then headed on down the road toward Terra Mall.

Before they got there, Ben asked, "Can we see where Jesus is teaching?"

Cal was the one who responded from behind the wheel. "I'm not that familiar with this area. We'd probably better stick to the original plan."

Lydia concurred. "We don't know how safe it would be for Jesus to be greeting people in that neighborhood."

The sign for the mall appeared ahead on the left, and Calvin took the exit ramp directly on the right. They found themselves passing a neighborhood soccer field and a row of small businesses. The road dipped and they slowed down as several cars entered their path from a tunnel on the left. Ahead there seemed to be some sort of intersection where a bus had stopped and people were getting off. Some were walking to the right and others were getting on a pedestrian overpass which bridged the highway they had just left.

As they got to the intersection, they realized that there was no turn to the left. The only direction they could go was right. So, that is the way that they turned. Past a couple of churches and a whole string of various businesses, they finally came to an intersection. Ahead on the left was a small grocery store. Right in front of the store was a turn into a gated community, though the gate stood open and unguarded.

Ben grabbed Gretchen's arm. "Do you see what I see?"

Gretchen strained to look. "Was that our friends the Workmans?"

"Our friend, at least," said Ben. "I thought I saw Harry, but not Kitty."

Cal pulled over to the right as far as he could without going into the ditch. "I'm not sure where this road is leading. It seems to be headed away from the mall."

Gretchen looked at her son and at Lydia. "Could we drive the other way slowly to see if we do see our friends?"

Lydia was frowning. "Why would your friends be in this neighborhood?"

Ben chuckled. "Maybe they had the same problem we are having finding the mall."

Lydia thought that sounded reasonable.

Cal jacked the car back and forth on the narrow road until he had turned around. He got a little flustered because his maneuver blocked the path of a passing bus for a minute. The bus honked and pedestrians were laughing at his attempt to turn around.

Ben patted his son on the back. "I'm glad you're driving and not me," he said.

Calvin replied through his teeth. "I wish we had Jesus or Jaime back."

They finally got their car going in the opposite direction, and a few seconds later they saw their friend again.

Harry Workman was talking to two young women a little way down a side street. More exactly, Harry was talking to a young woman with a girl in school uniform standing a few feet away.

Calvin turned into the side street and pulled to the curb. This side street was actually wider than the street they had turned from, but it dead-ended a couple of blocks ahead. The three talking people glanced their way. Gretchen had the window down and stuck her hand out to wave. The girl in uniform turned away quickly, but the other two stared.

"Harry," Gretchen called. "Hi, Harry, what are you doing here?

"Must be lost," mumbled Ben from the other side of the car. He opened the door before Lydia could add a word of caution.

He was still within earshot when Lydia said, "Remember why Jesus is here."

Ben's steps slowed as he moved toward his former parishioner. Harry Workman appeared to be looking for a place to hide. The woman he had been talking to had her hand in her purse in a gesture which Ben felt unexplainably threatening. The school girl appeared to be studying a crack in the sidewalk very intently. Ben stopped about ten feet from Harry and the woman.

Harry tried to smile and look relaxed. "Oh, Pastor Ben, I'd forgotten you were coming to Costa Rica, too. It's great to see you."

Ben frowned. "It's good to see you, too, Harry, but I didn't expect to see you here. And where's Kitty?"

Harry looked uncomfortable. "She's at the mall over there." He nodded in the direction of Terra Mall. "I decided to go exploring."

"Is this young woman helping you find your way back?" Ben asked. "Maybe she can help us too." As he finished these words, he took a good look at the woman standing next to Harry. Back in the van, all three people noticed how Ben's spine straightened as he recognized her. "Excuse me," he said, addressing her with a smile, all the while remembering that hand still in her purse, "You look a lot like a lady I met earlier in our visit in this country. But, I just met her once, so I am not sure..."

"You too look familiar, *señor*," replied the woman. "I sometimes work in the airport. Could we have seen each other there?"

Ben frowned and shook his head. "I can't remember for sure. But my memory is that you were someone who tried to make visitors like us welcome."

As these words left Ben's mouth, Harry staggered, almost falling. Ben noticed another person approaching them; he glanced that way and saw Jesus frowning, staring beyond him, and slowly shaking his head. Ben realized now, if he had had any lingering doubt, that his "friend" had been found in the middle of an immoral transaction. He focused on Harry, "Harry you can come with us, we can go to the mall together and find Kitty."

Harry hesitated, glancing around him nervously, and noticed Jesus coming down the hill toward the group. The woman saw the change in his expression and turned to face Jesus herself. She acted like she recognized Jesus immediately and grabbed Harry, pulling him between herself and Jesus. The hand had come out of her purse and did hold a gun. The school girl started to run away from Jesus when she saw the woman's reaction.

In a split second Lydia was out of the van and running down the girl. When she had grabbed the girl, Lydia maneuvered them both behind the van so they were somewhat protected from the nervous woman's weapon. Gretchen saw that holding the girl would keep Lydia from being able to help with the rest of the situation, so she also got out of the van. With a quick move which surprised the other two, Gretchen took charge of holding the school girl in a half nelson. Then she pushed the girl into the van. The school bag dropped, and the girl was positioned on the floor of the van. Lydia turned her attention back to the scene down the street, with both Calvin and Gretchen watching the girl.

Suddenly Ben, who had moved to one side so that he was not in a line with the woman and Jesus, stood up straight and pointed at Harry's chest. In a booming voice, which rivaled the loudest of the celebrity preachers, he said, "Harry Workman, you are a sinner – caught in the act by God and by me. Repent and kneel before your God -- or DIE."

It wasn't clear whether Harry dropped to his knees in response to Ben's words, or just collapsed. The woman made an effort to hold him, but had not been holding him in a way that could control a dead weight. She was still grabbing at him when Jesus closed in on her. As she pulled up her gun toward Jesus, there was a loud sharp sound and the woman crumpled. Ben could tell from a whooshing past his ear that it had been Lydia, rather than Jesus who had shot the prostitution recruiter.

Inside the van, Gretchen and Cal tried to keep their focus on the teenager who was now weeping on the floor of the van. Harry crouched shivering on the pavement while a pool of blood spread from the woman lying close to him.

Jesus talked rapidly into his phone while Lydia, who had somehow gotten plastic gloves on her hands, ripped off the woman's shirt and used it to apply pressure to a wound in the woman's back.

The next hour passed in a combination of slow motion and hyper speed. Every second took an eternity, but it took no time at all for drug police and emergency personnel to appear and take over. Lydia disinfected her hands thoroughly after she removed her gloves. Then she found some fresh clothes and changed in the back of the van. Cleansing her hands one final time, she took in the situation in the van.

Gretchen and Cal were straightening things up after the police had taken away both Harry and the girl. Ben and Jesus had gone with other officers to find Mrs. Workman.

A small car zipped past them from inside the gated community. A distraught woman and an angry looking man were its occupants. "God help that couple," prayed Gretchen. "If they are that girl's parents, give them wisdom and courage to handle the situation in the best way possible."

CHAPTER 19

Gretchen found herself filled with mixed feelings as she waited in line to check in at Juan Santamaria airport. She and Ben were finally returning home, just a few days later than their originally scheduled flight, and with an upgrade to first class for their return. She was going to miss Calvin terribly, and she was going to miss Jesus almost as much. Lydia was going to continue "guarding" them as far as Miami; then they would lose her company too. She glanced at Ben. He looked very tired. They both felt relief at the thought of sleeping that night in their own beds at home. They would enjoy the secure feeling of recognizing where they were when they awoke the next morning.

****

Calvin, Gretchen, and Lydia had joined Jesus and Ben at the mall shortly after they had found Kitty. It ended up that police officers drove both the Workman's car and the SUV the others had been driving to the downtown station. Kitty, Gretchen, and Ben rode in Kitty's car; most of the time during the drive was spent comforting Kitty who was still trying to comprehend what had happened. She had thought her husband was having digestive issues and spending a lot of time in the mall's restroom until the police approached her. Though Gretchen and Ben had questions for each other, those had to wait.

After they had finally left Kitty in her hotel room, very white and weary, they settled in a room of their own down the hall. Cal and Jesus were sharing a room on one side of them and Lydia was across the hall.

Gretchen settled into a stuffed chair by their bed,

while Ben collapsed into the middle of the bed itself. She turned her head toward her husband and said, "I'm tired, but I have questions. Can I ask them?"

Ben was staring at the ceiling. "I've got questions too, so let's take turns. You first."

"Well, I guess I'll start with when you realized what Harry was doing. When was that?"

Ben sighed. "Did you see my walk start to slow as I approached Harry?"

Gretchen nodded, "I noticed."

"Lydia's words about why Jesus was there were sinking in. I looked at Harry and he looked more scared than happy to see me. The young girl was trying to be invisible, and the woman, the ... Well, she had her hand in her purse, but wasn't rummaging around or pulling the hand out. My first intention was to go up and shake my friend's hand. I think I'm glad I didn't, though I wish ..."

Gretchen waited a moment, then said, "Your turn."

"Gretchen, what happened behind me when the girl ran?"

"Lydia caught her. My training at the reform school years ago came in handy – I took over guarding the girl, with Cal's help. We held her on the floor of the van while Lydia positioned herself behind the van's front bumper. I couldn't see everything while we were guarding the girl, but one or the other of us would keep a lookout and tell the other most things.

"I had been praying that you would move somehow so that you weren't between Lydia and the rest of them. You didn't know where Lydia was, what made you move?"

Ben chuckled. "Inspiration. And ... I didn't want to be shot accidentally by Jesus. I was actually moving out of his path."

"Well, that bring us to your little ... err ... preacher outburst. Jesus was approaching; Lydia was in position. The woman saw Jesus and grabbed Harry."

"I remembered that Harry always cringed at loud noises. I was hoping he would cringe **and** listen to my words. And I hoped that approach would be outside the woman's language and cultural understanding of us *Norte Americanos*. I doubt she watches too many television preachers."

Gretchen agreed, but said nothing.

Ben inhaled deeply. "I didn't expect my words to give Harry a heart attack."

Gretchen reached over and put a comforting arm on her husband. "They aren't sure yet that it actually was a heart attack, honey. Anyway, I think he might be glad that he's spending the night in the hospital rather than a jail cell."

Ben hit the bed with one arm. "The one I feel for is Kitty. What a shock!"

"And to be put in the position of having to support his pain while in such emotional pain yourself!" added Gretchen.

Another sigh from Ben. "At least Harry asked for forgiveness."

"Yes, he did." agreed Gretchen. "Again and again and again. Kitty was getting irritated at his asking."

"When you and Kitty went to *el baño*, I told Harry to stop; that he couldn't expect her to be ready to forgive him immediately. He swore it was the first time he'd done any-thing like that. I don't know whether to believe him or not. You don't just end up in a strange neighborhood in a strange country making a deal for a prostitute unless … unless you've spent some time preparing for that moment."

"That's for Harry, Kitty, God, and the authorities to figure out," responded Gretchen. "You saved his life; it is not yours to save his soul."

"And you are not responsible for Kitty; though I'm sure God put you in position to help her through this initial phase."

"I've already mentioned the name of the lady counselor who helped me during that rough spell I had when you were pastor of their church."

"Good. And her husband might be able to work with Harry – if he's allowed to leave the country."

In the room across the hall, Jesus and Cal and Lydia were visiting.

"I was so scared that there would be a gun battle with Ben caught in the middle." declared Jesus.

"So was I," murmured Lydia.

Cal championed his father. "Dad seems to have a sixth sense about these things, or divine guidance. I've seen him seem perfectly clueless about a situation, yet ask the perfect question or say the perfect thing."

"Or make the perfect sidestep," added Jesus.

"Divine guidance," murmured Lydia.

Jesus turned in his chair so that he faced Lydia completely. "Lydia, we both face danger like we experienced today repeatedly in our jobs. If things had gone badly today – if that woman had gotten that gun out of her purse and shot me – I know that I would have been OK. If I had been killed, I would have gone to heaven. Do you have that assurance?"

Lydia looked down at her hands as she rubbed them together. "I don't know... I try to be a good person ... I try to help make the world a better place with my job ..." She looked back at Jesus. "But ... no, I do not have any assurance about what would happen to me."

"God does not play games with us about such a serious thing, Lydia," responded Jesus. "He does not sit back in heaven saying, 'I am going to keep those little humans guessing as to whether I have accepted them.' He loves us and does not want to turn us away from heaven."

Cal cleared his throat. "I'm not that good at talking about these things, but I remember Bible verses Mom and Dad made me learn as a child. One is this: 'Not by works of righteousness which we have done, but according to His mercy He saves us, by the washing of regeneration and renewing of the Holy Ghost.' That's the old King James version of Titus 3:5, but the meaning is there. We can't be good enough on our own. Only God's mercy – his cleansing of our souls stained from evil – can save us, can help us to become what God intended us to be."

Jesus nodded. "*Exactamente*, Calvin. In the Bible book of Isaiah, chapter 53, it reminds us that we all have 'gone astray, We have turned everyone to his own way...' That is where Jesus comes in – not me, but the Son of God. He died to pay the penalty for our sins, and He rose to show that He was victorious over sin and death. In mass, we pray for the peace of God to be upon us. The only way we can have that peace is to know that we have accepted what Jesus has done for us. To know that we are right with God, not because of what we have done, but because of what Jesus has done."

Lydia felt unexplainably light-hearted. She didn't have to keep trying by herself; she could count on God – she could trust God. In fact, He had already done what was needed to give her peace.

She knew that life would still contain many problems, but she was going to have that joy – that assurance – that God cared. The resistance she had felt so long against religious things was gone. It had been caused, she realized now, by anger at God. But God hadn't harmed her; He had wanted to help her a long time before she was even born. The questions weren't all answered, but she saw clearly now that good and evil were two separate forces. She also understood finally what she had always hoped was true: that God's goodness was much stronger than evil. Only such a great power would be willing to sacrifice what Jesus had sacrificed, and she was going to be stronger now that she was joining that power.
***

Lost in their own thoughts, Ben and Gretchen finally

got to the check-in counter in the airport. After they and Lydia had checked in, they were led through an expedited security section and hurried to a VIP room near their gate.

Left alone, Ben spoke. "I hope Harry has learned his lesson. I'm glad he won't be tried for a crime here in Costa Rica because of his heart condition, but ..."

"But he will never be allowed back in the country, either," Lydia reminded him. "He is permanently banned."

"Something needed to happen to him," Gretchen commented grimly. "Loose ends have been tied up about as much as they can be, except for one."

"Agreed," replied Lydia, "There has been a domino of arrests around Costa Rica in the last week. Just one missing teenager."

Ben looked sad. "The one from Jesus' friend's church."

All were quiet for a while. Lydia glanced at her friends and realized that their heads were bowed in prayer. She decided to join them; it couldn't hurt, and she felt like she and God were on better terms than they had been. He might listen to her, also.

The door opened and they were called to board the plane. Gretchen and Ben found their seats 5A and 5B and quickly got settled. Lydia was behind them in 6A. Others were settling into the other first class seats. A distinguished-looking middle-aged man came in almost dragging a sullen, heavy-eyed teenager. Both looked Latin, but the man spoke in perfect U.S. English to the flight attendant. "My daughter has been feeling badly for several days. She is actually feeling better now; no fever, but she is very tired."

The attendant was sympathetic and went to get pillows and a blanket for the girl. While the attendant was going, the girl said something that Gretchen over-heard by accident. Though the girl's speech was slurred, Gretchen was pretty sure that she had heard correctly:

"Daughter ... I am not your daughter ... I am not ... I

don't like you."

Gretchen's hand tightened on her husband's arm. Ben looked at her with a question in his face. Gretchen signaled him to be quiet and listen.

The man laughed nervously. "I know that you are unhappy with me right now, but you will be happy when we get to the U.S. You will have a very pampered life. You will be rich."

Ben's mouth dropped open.

Another attendant came up the aisle. "*Señor* Camron, you need to get your bags and your daughter's out of the walkway."

The man got up and started searching for a place to stow the bags. As he moved down the center of the plane, Gretchen leaned forward and spoke the name *Miranda* in a low voice. The girl looked up at her clearly in response to that name. She turned toward Ben who appeared to be ahead of her. "I guess I need a trip down the aisle," he said with a wink. As soon as he was gone, Gretchen motioned Lydia to join her.

Quickly she explained what she had seen and heard. Lydia pulled out her cell phone, got up, and strode through the curtains dividing first class from coach. When she got back, both Ben and Gretchen were waiting for some kind of report. Lydia had a message written on her smart phone, it said:

Identities confirmed. Team wants arrest in Miami. Flight crew in loop. Extra marshals on board.

Needless to say, Gretchen and Ben had a hard time concentrating on the in-flight movie. As they taxied into the Miami airport, the flight attendants moved quietly up and down the rows of seats asking if anyone had seen a lost passport. When they got to Gretchen and Ben, the two saw that, contrary to their words, the important message was written on a small piece of paper. It said, "Please stay seated for a minute while we exit a special needs passenger first."

As they rolled into position and the ramp was locked into place, one attendant bent over the man and girl in seats 4A and 4B. "We see that your daughter is still feeling badly. We will let you exit the aircraft first, so that you can get her to a comfortable place."

"Oh, that isn't necessary," replied the man.

But the attendant was already motioning him to get up.

Through a small crack between the plane and the ramp, Ben caught a glimpse of a uniform. They heard a slight commotion as air marshals closed in behind the two. By the time they exited, a group of officers had the man handcuffed and in custody. On the opposite side of the walkway, two women, one in uniform and one with a stethoscope, were helping the girl.

Lydia said a brief, but sincere, good-by to the Parks and hurried off in the direction of the police officers. That was the last they saw of her as they made their way to the next flight's gate. When they got to the St. Louis airport, television monitors were running a news report about Chicago millionaire Philip Camron being arrested for human trafficking.

Gretchen noticed the bathroom used on their initial visit, now about two and a half weeks ago. She motioned and they took turns, like they had on their first trip, even repeating their dances to relieve tension.

When they finally got back to the little airport where their adventure began, Gretchen saw that her fellow teacher was there working her second job again. She blushed when she saw Gretchen. "How was your trip?" she asked.

"It was a once-in-a-lifetime experience," Ben replied.

Gretchen nodded. "Costa Rica is a remarkable country," she said. "We made some new friends."

Teacher/TSA worker Amanda raised her eyebrows, but all she said was "I'm glad it ended better than it began."

Ben reached for Gretchen's hand. They were both

thinking of the girl who would now have a second chance for a normal life.

"Much better," responded Gretchen.

ABOUT THE AUTHOR

Kathy Carman Henderson considers her life an adventure of its own. She was born in the Philippines, raised in Central Kansas, and has spent her adult life following her husband's pastoral career through Iowa and Illinois. She has a husband, children, grandchildren, and a church family who are all important to her. In addition, she has been privileged to work in a variety of jobs caring for children. Her current one is as a teacher of the gifted and talented. Though this book is fiction, she set it in the location of one of her personal adventures and has chosen to address an issue important to her.

Look for future adventures of Ben & Gretchen in the Grand Canyon, Florida, and the Philippines.

Isaiah 58:6
"Is this not the fast which I choose,
To loosen the bonds of wickedness,
To undo the bands of the yoke,
And to let the oppressed go free
And break every yoke?"
NASB

Made in the USA
Lexington, KY
09 December 2012